24

)

.ed, riveting book that you won't want to put down until you get to the last page and then you'll be wanting more. This book would be great for anyone who likes friends to more to enemies to more, second chances, suspense, twists, and action."

—Jean, GOODREADS

"Get ready for a fast-paced, action-packed read involving running from the militia, being shot at, surviving falling into the river, battling a wildfire, and getting people to safety. If you enjoy a heart-pounding suspense read with danger, rivals, and second chances, you'll enjoy *Burning Rivals*."

—Allyson, GOODREADS

"Wow. Another nail-biting adventure full of suspense, mystery and emotion. This book mad me laugh out loud, cry, and had me on the edge of my seat. How it tied into the first book is incredible. Definitely another must read!"

—Heather, GOODREADS

"I enjoyed being back in Alaska fighting fires with the crew. My favorite part of this book was how the team supported each other not only on the job but also as they lived out their faith!!"

BURNING RIVALS

BURNING RIVALS

VONI HARRIS

sunrise
PUBLISHING

Burning Rivals
Chasing Fire: Alaska, Book 2

For more information about Voni Harris, please access the author's website at voniharris.com
Published in the United States of America.
Cover Design: Sunrise Media Group LLC

· CHASING FIRE ALASKA ·

BURNING HEARTS
BURNING RIVALS
BURNING ESCAPE
BURNING SECRETS
BURNING TRUTH
BURNING JUSTICE

My sister, Kirsti, is a God-lover
and a fighter, and I will keep learning that
from her my entire life.

Some trust in chariots and some in horses, but we trust in the name of the LORD our God.

PSALM 20:7ESV

ONE

CADEE MOORE HAD NEVER RUN FROM a fight, and running today might well cost her life.

"Thirty seconds to jump!" Neil, their pilot, called back from the cockpit of the Midnight Sun smokejumping plane.

In all her years of being a hotshot, and now a smokejumper, Cadee Moore had never run from gunmen on ATVs to a plane, been shot at as the plane took off... or known for certain their plane was going to crash.

She gripped the armrests.

In the front row next to Vince Ramos, she could see past him out the window to where smoke billowed from each engine. The plane shook hard, bucked side to side. Her stomach swished around with it.

God!

She reached down and pulled out her parachute and her fire pack from under her seat.

Jumping from a plane streaming smoke was not a thing she'd ever expected as a smokejumper. She twisted the tracker ring Jade had given all the Midnight Sun SJs.

They'd barely made it off the ground before guns had begun shooting at the plane.

They had parachutes, and they had a pilot still doing his best to get them as high as possible and as far as possible from the militiamen.

But the crash was going to happen.

Vince adjusted the straps of his fire pack on his lap and shot her the hard glance she'd lately grown accustomed to, frowning, his dark eyebrows meeting in the middle. Because he thought she was scared?

He called out, "Hey, Jade, I'll just go down by myself, all right?"

"We're both going down. We're supposed to pair off. What is your problem?" Okay, she sounded just as antagonistic as he had.

Jade leaned into their space, her brown eyes blazing. Her voice was scarily steady and quiet. "The two of you and your constant bickering is why I assigned you as partners." She sighed.

"You jump first. Together." She stood straight. "You're grownups. Work. It. Out. Have each other's backs." Her dark-blonde braid swung as she turned to help Logan adjust his chute.

Cadee and Vince looked at each other. He dipped his head to her, and she returned it. She would have his back. It seemed like he'd have hers. She focused her attention on her own chute.

What is his problem anyway?

No matter how hard he pushed, she couldn't back down until she knew *why* he treated her like this.

The rest of the Midnight Sun crew was, well . . . neutral toward her.

Vince . . . not so much. He was never anything but angry at her. Never did anything but dig into her.

At one time, she and Vince had dated. They'd been in love, and she'd thought it would last forever. Until he'd broken it off. For no reason she understood.

These days she didn't understand Vince at all.

The plane tilted nose first, and they screamed toward the earth . . . for a second or two. But Neil was a top-notch pilot.

She quickly patted over her fire pack, even though she'd already triple-checked it.

"Now! Go now!" Saxon, the spotter, called over his shoulder from the cockpit.

Cadee jumped up, stepped into her fire pack, and popped into the aisle. She adjusted her bright orange Nomex fire jacket and put on her helmet. Well, she called it a head cage.

Behind her, Vince tugged at her parachute.

She turned and tugged at his straps. They fist-bumped. Trusting Vince was not the issue. This was the man she'd dated while they were in the Ember training program together. The man for whom her feelings were still alive. Even if she would never admit it.

Jade opened the hatch, and Cadee stood in the opening.

Thump, thump. Jade tapped her shoulders, and Cadee jumped out of the plane.

The noise of the wind filled her ears as she fell through the air. The chute opened, popped her up. Now she was floating, not falling, and there was peaceful quiet.

Or at least, there soon would be.

She teared up at the whine of the plane falling. Other smokejumpers fell out, and she prayed their chutes caught them. The red-and-white aircraft dipped toward the ground in front of her.

It streamed with smoke, flipped, then hit the ground.

Flames exploded into the air.

Fighting the toggles, she twisted her head and counted parachutes. The wind seemed to be separating them all over the place, but she spotted everyone. *Thank God.* "God, protect the SJs. Please. Please." The mossy forest below was a beautiful soft green dotted by fireweed and other wildflowers, but she couldn't enjoy the view. She was squinting, looking for ATVs.

Vince was close, floating down with her.

Since Vince had been brought onto Midnight Sun this season, they hadn't even had short conversations. Just fights. She was so tired of it. When Jade had made them partners, it'd gotten even worse. She didn't even know Vince anymore. Worse, when he was around, she didn't know *herself* anymore either.

But they were supposed to work together. Jade was right. Bickering would get them both killed—and maybe everyone else on the team as well.

She wrestled the toggles. Cadee looked down at the spruce trees reaching up to them, swaying. This was a crazy wind.

And who knew what was going to happen? The

militia wanted them all dead. Those guys with guns were probably down there waiting for them.

God!

She scanned the ridgeline. The valley floor. And a jolt of recognition shook through her.

Cadee knew about where she and Vince were. She'd grown up around here.

Ingriq Village was at least fifteen miles to the southeast. She could already see the ribbon of the river where she and her sister, Emma, had spent countless hours. The paved road from the village to Copper Mountain cut through the beauty of the land.

And at the end of that road . . . safety.

If they could outrun the guys with the guns.

The last thing Vince Ramos wanted was his life in Cadee Moore's hands.

He held his steering lines tight, but the air shifted so hard they were nearly useless.

If he'd believed God was in control, he might've thanked Him for the parachute. But the wind might still kill him. Was God going to take care of that? He hadn't taken care of the Midnight Sun crew's plane. Or the adrenaline of surviving the crash.

It was parachutes that had taken care of the team—he hoped.

They'd at least taken care of himself and Cadee. So far.

But it was the parachutes, not God.

And he and Cadee would have to somehow deal with the partnership Jade had forced them into, as well as with their conflict. And they'd have to do it *themselves*.

Vince looked over at her. Her creamy skin had turned ruddy, and her dark-brown ponytail with blonde highlights was chaos. She was battling the wind too, and handling it well. But as soon as they reached the ground, there would be no more peaceful quiet.

The training at the extra-tough Ember, Montana, smokejumping program had been a test of his skills. Cadee's too. They had both pursued that training because they knew Alaska would be a tough place to serve, and they'd both been gunning for the Midnight Sun SJ crew. But Ember was where the training program was run by those legendary smokejumpers that people wrote books about. Jed Ransom. Tucker Newman—now their commander.

Still, his only goal had been coming to Alaska.

Vince had been in college when Dad had become the Midnight Sun smokejumper boss, and he'd wanted to learn from that man. And get away from his DEA job.

Cadee had grown up in Alaska, and her heart was here. They'd both finished the training course, but she'd completed it slightly ahead of him—and Midnight Sun had only had one slot.

The bosses had given it to Cadee, and she'd gone home. He'd stayed in Montana and worked last year's fire season as a smokejumper in Ember while she'd been in Alaska, working under his father.

Nine months ago, his dad had died at the Aktuvik fire.

He stopped that thought process to focus on steering through the harsh wind.

He finally saw a very small meadow surrounded by Sitka spruce up ahead. The wind was thankfully sending them that direction. He pointed at it, shouted over to Cadee.

When the ground finally showed up, he rolled to his knees. He stood up, gathered his chute fast, and ran to the edge of the meadow to make room for her to land.

Wait.

Where was Cadee?

He turned a three sixty, seeing only moss, grass, trees. "Cadee!" he shouted.

"Stupid wind blew me into this spruce, Vince," she called.

He looked up, shrugged out of his parachute straps, and ran over as fast as he could.

"You didn't land a perfect jump, did you?" He shook his head to clear his stupidity. He hadn't meant for it to come out that way. He didn't know why every word that issued from his mouth around her was antagonistic. Why did he always act like this near her?

Right.

He knew why. This was the woman who had cost him his father.

He stood under the tree and looked up to see the mess the wind had made for her. He saw how to get her down. "Just a minute. I've got you."

"Are you serious?" Cadee twisted around gently, looking up and examining how the parachute cord had trapped her in the tree. "I'm fine. I can take care of myself, thank you very much."

He opened his mouth to respond. Closed it. He'd probably deserved that, the way he'd been laying into her lately.

She reached up and took hold of the thick limb she was hanging from with both hands, swung her legs once, twice. The third time, her legs grabbed the limb, and she pulled herself up.

Okay, he had some abs, but this reminded him to level up his core exercises. A couple levels.

"Great job. I'll help . . ."

She glared down at him and stood on the limb.

Fine. He closed his mouth again and just stood and watched.

Cadee pulled out her pocketknife from her flight pack and cut the parachute cords, taking her time to untangle them from the branches where needed. She gathered the parachute, then, sitting on the limb like it was a chair, she stuffed the chute into her pack.

She stepped down the broken moss-covered branches like the spruce was nothing more than a ladder.

Of course.

Almost to the ground, she pushed away from the trunk and landed next to him. "So, I saw that everyone got out of the plane. About where did any of them land?"

He shook his head. "No idea."

"Really? You stood there watching me instead of assessing our situation?"

"I was watching your back in case something bad happened."

Her jaw jutted out. "Like I'm incapable? Untrained? Just a 'guurrl,' like you said the other day when I couldn't lift the huge boulder by myself at the fire? Jade and Skye and I got it out of the way. All of us 'guurrls.'"

He closed one eye, staring at her with the other. Her bright blue eyes were blazing right back at him. That spirit was what he'd always loved about her. Until his anger at her. "Part of being a team is watching your teammate's back. I was *trying* to watch your back."

She huffed.

It did sound awful, the things he'd said, hearing them from her voice. "I didn't mean you are an incapable woman." It wasn't what he thought of her anyway. "I knew I couldn't have lifted it myself, and that's just a way my dad made Mom laugh when she asked him to lift something around the house."

"Fine. I could see that from him."

"Let's do an assessment." He pulled out his phone. "Seventy-one degrees, zero percent humidity." He pointed to the right at the skinny plume of smoke. "Plane crash there."

He ran his hand through his hair. Glanced at Cadee, who was studying the ground.

She slowly met his gaze, her eyes glistening. "If Neil didn't make it . . . his wife . . ."

"Neil—he's the best." He swallowed hard.

She nodded. Then she took a deep breath. "Anyway, look," she said. She pointed into the sky. "Heavy bird traffic coming our way. The smoke's moving this direction, thanks to that wind. Fast. The plane crash has started a wildfire."

He scanned the horizon above the soaring spruce trees. It wasn't just smoke from a tiny campfire. It was fanning out through the sky. "You're dead right."

"It's headed toward the village," she said, her voice tight.

"What village?"

"I know it's there." She took off running toward the wildfire.

"Cadee!" he shouted. "We can't fight the fire ourselves. Without tools. Without teammates."

She stopped. Didn't turn around.

"Listen. Like it or not, we are teammates. And right now, all we have is each other. We need to work together."

She turned around. "You're right. I'll be the guide. Which means you need to *keep up.*"

His jaw clenched. "Cadee. I've got a map. I've

got a compass. We'll get to the jump base, get the rest of the team together, get to the fire."

Was her face red in anger? Or red from the coolish air of the Alaskan summer?

"We don't have time to gather the team. We have to head to Ingriq Village."

What? He stood his ground. "Why? No. We need to head to base, not wander around."

"Ingriq needs us. Now. It's close to the fire. We need to warn them, get them out of there."

He shook his head. "Let's get back to base, and we can send out a crew to warn them."

"It won't be soon enough! We're going to run out of time!"

"And we have people on our tail trying to kill us! We need to get out of here—now!" His voice lowered. "Come on, Cadee. Work with me."

"I can't. I know this village. I have to warn them. Before it's too late."

Her tone made his heart squeeze in his chest. Her face had paled when she'd seen the smoke rising above the forest.

"I get that. I really do. But what if these guys find us and we bring trouble to the village? We need to get to the authorities right now. Listen, when we get into range, we can call it in."

"No." And her voice even shook a little. "That's

my village. Those are my people. Stay here if you want, but I'm going."

He could kick himself. She hadn't just grown up in Alaska, she'd grown up *here*. "You were raised in Ingriq Village?"

She nodded. "We have to get there, Vince. Fast."

"Family there?"

"My sister. Niece." She huffed. "My niece is four. She has asthma."

Ah. A child with asthma and a wildfire. Not good. He could kick himself again. The fire's expected behavior was obvious at the moment.

"Your dad taught us that people always come first."

His mouth tightened. Really? She had to bring up his father? But that was why Vince had become a DEA agent—before he'd wised up and chosen to listen to God's call to wildland firefighting.

Now he was a firefighter for the exact same reason.

"Okay. Fine. I'll try to call Jade and Tucker. You text the rest." Standard Firefighting Order.

She nodded, started punching at her phone.

He pulled out his phone and called Jade. The service only lasted one second, then cut off. Same thing happened the next two times he tried. Then he tried to call Tucker Newman, the base commander, but he didn't answer either. Vince left a message. "No answer, phone call or text."

Cadee punched hard at her phone, scowled at it, gave up, and stuck it in her pocket. "I'll text them as soon as we get to coverage. God, please keep the crew safe."

She really thought that? He scowled. "God isn't going to help us. He doesn't show up."

Her jaw dropped open so far it practically fell to the ground. "Really? You were always such a strong believer. It was part of the reason I never lost hope the past year, because I knew *you* wouldn't. God might not have shown up in the exact way I wanted Him to all the time, but I *always* knew He was there."

He'd left that childish part of his life behind when his father died, thank you. "Whatever."

"Ingriq is that way, Vince. Let's go." She pointed to the east.

"Yeah. What's the fastest way? We need the map."

She narrowed her eyes but stepped beside him, looked at the map. She poked her finger. "Here's where we are." Then another finger poke. "There's the village."

"So, a river between here and there." His finger traced it.

"Yeah. Not far away, I'm guessing. I've been to that river a lot, and I visited the area between here and there." She sighed. "But not often, and it was a long time ago."

He folded the map and put it in his fire pack. Really? So she'd been here a lot. He swallowed, forcing the frustration out of his voice. "Hard to tell on the map exactly what we'll see, but—"

The pop of a gunshot sounded through the meadow.

A bullet skimmed over his left shoulder.

Vince slammed into Cadee as all his old DEA training rushed back. The heat of gunfire. A civilian in danger.

He lay over her, protecting her from bullets.

Had the militia found them?

TWO

CADEE LAY FLAT ON THE GROUND behind the fallen spruce tree, practically buried in the forest litter. Underneath Vince.

She could feel his heartbeat pounding.

Like the pound of his heartbeat during their Ember training—her last day. They'd had to run three miles in forty-five minutes carrying 150 pounds. Every training. Every day. But on her last day, she'd *finally* beaten him, his sweaty hug her reward.

Today, though, was like a switch had flipped in him, some sort of ingrained training.

"What's going on? You okay?" she whispered.

He shushed her, hard.

A spruce cone poked into her cheek. Deeply.

But she lay still, quiet, absorbing the warmth of Vince. He smelled of fresh air. And sweat.

A junco bird in the spruce tree above them rat-a-tatted his song.

Vince rolled off her. Her breath was trying to rupture her lungs, her nerves buzzed. But she dared not move.

For . . . forever, it felt like.

Maybe actually two minutes. Or five. She kept herself from even looking at her watch.

She peered over Vince's shoulder. "I see him. There's a guy on an ATV. Just like the ATV we were running from to get the crew on the plane with Jamie and Tristan."

Beside her, Vince hissed, "Stay down!"

"Let's run for real cover."

"No!" He cut his voice down to a low rumble against her ear. "If we stand up right now, the four-wheeler creeps will mow us down. Stay put."

"Why are they after us?"

"Maybe the militia put a hit out on all of the smokejumpers."

"Because . . ."

"Maybe to get to Jamie Winters, Logan's friend. She stole an SD card from their camp. I heard them talking. She copied all their financials on it."

"And because of that, they shot down our plane and are still trying to kill us?"

He blew out a breath, shook his head. "You have no idea what kind of people are out here. Or what they'll do."

She stilled. And he did?

Vince peeked his head just above the trunk of the spruce. Then he rose to his knees, swiveling his head. "The ATVs are gone. I think we're okay now." He stood up. Held out his hand to help her.

Cadee picked herself up off the ground, knocked the spruce cone stuck to her cheek.

"You okay?" he asked, his voice still low.

"I'm fine." She brushed the dirt off her knees, her hands. "Are you hit?"

And just like that, an ATV roared into the clearing. Another shot. This time, over Cadee's head.

"*Run*!" he shouted.

She took off toward the river.

Vince right behind her, she zigzagged from one tall spruce tree trunk to another.

Behind them, the ATVs crashed through the undergrowth.

These guys were gaining on them.

Where could they hide? Under the thick

growth of salmonberry bushes? She twisted her head, looking for a good growth.

Ahead, the roar of the river rose, and that meant one thing.

"Caves—we can hide in the caves!"

"Right!" Vince shouted.

"This way!" She grabbed at Vince and took a sharp left, up a hill.

A minute later, she and Vince pulled up short at the cliff that looked down into the quarter-mile-wide river, some twenty feet below—rushing white water, foamy, lethal. She scanned down the cliff on their side . . . there. She pointed at the black void, just below a jutting of rocks. "See that cave?"

Vince looked. "Yep."

"We'll pretend we're jumping into the river. Throw off these guys on the ATVs."

"Go down a cliff? I've got rope." He started looking into his fire pack.

"But we don't want to leave the rope hanging where they can tell where we are. You're a climber. This is a cave my sister and I climbed down to. It's doable."

"You what?" He shook his head. "Never mind. Okay."

"How do we make it look like we jumped?"

She glanced over her shoulder. Had they really outrun them, or just forced them to go the long way and bought a few seconds?

"We could tear one of our shirts on the salmonberries and leave it? Maybe add blood?"

"I'm not shedding any blood for this."

"Yeah, me neither." He already had his hands in his fire pack, and he pulled out a shirt. He walked over to a salmonberry bush and pushed hard. The twig caught it, ripped it, and he pulled it off.

With a quick grin, she pulled a couple salmonberries off and smeared their red juice on it.

She stuck one in her mouth, then they jogged up to the cliff, and Vince draped his shirt on the baby spruce angling out over the river.

She lowered herself over the cliff, climbed over the ledge, and swung into the cave.

The sound of ATV engines grew louder.

Of course.

Vince came down slowly, testing for the cave opening.

"They're coming!" she whisper-shouted up at him. She grabbed his legs so he'd feel the cave opening. "Get down here!"

He rolled himself into the darkness of the cave. They scrambled to the back and sat against the wall. As her eyes adjusted, she could see some tree roots poking out of the rough black rock that made up the wall of the cave.

The ATVs—was it four or five?—rumbled above them. Cadee could feel the vibration of the engines, and her nose stung with the smell of their diesel fuel.

"Got this shirt. Looks like blood," an ATV driver shouted.

Vince looked over at her, nodded, a look of triumph in his eyes. She grinned back, nodded.

And for a second, just a flash, it felt like old times.

"I don't see them in the river," a voice called over the engine noise.

"We'll find them down the river. Let's go!"

Cadee held her breath as the ATVs drove away through the woodland.

Vince shifted up to a sit. "I'm ready to—"

She shushed Vince and whispered, "They could be lying in wait for us up there." But she sat up too, and offered him a fist bump.

He fist-bumped with a grin.

She wondered how long this rapport would last before their arguing started all over again.

Cadee wrapped her arms around her legs. Kind of cool in the cave. She stretched her neck from side to side, prayed silently. *Thank You, God, for this hiding place. Lure the ATVs away, keep them away.*

She looked up. Vince was staring at her, lips pursed. *Praying?* he mouthed.

Cadee nodded, remembering when they'd been dating and would join hands in prayer.

But clearly he didn't pray anymore.

This time, he shrugged and pulled off his backpack. "You've been here before, I'm guessing?"

She smiled. "I have. Emma and I would sneak out by this river with sandwiches when Dad was busy at work. A lot. He didn't know."

"You rebel."

"Yeah. Dad was the village's garbageman. His income was pathetic. And he didn't know how to handle his little bit of money. But it kept us alive, so Ingriq was our home."

He reached for his pack.

Vince pulled out his water bottle.

He couldn't believe Cadee's crazy plan had worked, but it did seem like the ATV riders thought they'd fallen over the cliff.

"Think they're gone," he said. He touched the light on his wristwatch. Good grief. They'd been in the cave for several hours.

He stood and stretched, then walked over to the opening and peeked out. Still light, although the sun had started to fall. Could be close to midnight. And in the distance, the sky fogged with smoke.

They needed to get moving.

He handed her the water bottle. "How far to the village?"

She reached into her leg pocket and tossed him a granola bar, opened one herself. "A couple miles as the crow flies. I know some paths that will cut the distance. You sure the ATVs are gone?"

"No. But they might have followed the river to the bridge. It's down about five miles, and they might've waited for us there."

"Makes sense. They'll want to make sure we're dead, right?"

Vince gave a grim nod. Then he reached for his pack, grimaced.

"You okay?"

He handed over her pack. "Fine." He walked to the opening of the cave.

It was awkward to look without falling, but with his back to the opening, he attempted to get a glimpse at the layout above them. Cadee had just reached up to the ground above them and started to lift herself up when rocks came tumbling down.

She dropped back into the cave.

"The edge is weak after the rain last night. If I lift you up, you can grab more than just the edge." At least he'd noticed that, taking a look at it.

"Right." She picked herself up off the floor of the cave.

He roughed the thick curls of his hair, picked up their packs, and tossed them up over the edge.

She wiped off the seat of her pants and pinched her lips together, looking out of the cave. She turned to him, her cheeks puffing with a breath. "Let's do it."

She'd listened to him? Wow.

He bit his tongue to keep from commenting and reached down to lift her up. She scrambled a bit and put both elbows up the edge of the land above them. He let go of her legs, and she pulled herself up. A couple seconds later, her head peeked over the edge, and she reached down both hands to him.

"Don't be silly. I'll pull you right over."

"Fine. Give me the rope. You can use that."

His rope. He pulled it out of his pack and tossed it up to her. She grabbed it, disappeared a moment, and then it fell down to him.

He used it to climb up the edge. "Good job."

She eyed him but didn't comment. So, that might be a win.

She coiled up the rope and added it to her pack, then pointed north, away from the river. "That way."

"On your six."

She smiled, and for a second, the sight of it stirred a memory, something sweet and perfect and . . .

Nope. That had been then. This was now. He pulled out his phone as he followed her through the brush.

He had one bar and tried Jade, but no response.

He tried it again.

Still no response.

"Good grief, Vince. Don't try every two seconds," Cadee snapped. "You'll run down your battery."

He bit back a response and slid his phone into his pocket.

He stepped over a spruce tree root curved above the ground like a whale breaching in the ocean. "Where are we going?"

"We're headed to the fireweed field and across it. Emma and I loved the fireweed, but it was too far to walk to without Mom and Dad." She looked over her shoulder at him. "We did anyway. Not frequently. Sometimes we didn't tell them school was letting out early, and we came out here together. Found the cave in the cliff. Hmmm . . . five miles. Now that I'm an adult, I can see why they wouldn't let us."

He laughed. "I'd never heard of Ingriq."

She elbowed him. "Of course not, with a population of one hundred forty-eight. Wait, Jane had a baby last month. One hundred forty-nine."

"Huh."

She hoisted herself over the trunk of a fallen spruce high above the ground. He wanted to help her, but he didn't dare. And she didn't need it.

He hauled himself over the spruce, behind her. "So, Cadee, I knew you lived in Alaska, but why didn't you ever tell me about growing up in Ingriq?"

Her silence felt like pressure in his ears. He started to ask again. No. She hadn't said anything about the village—but then again, he'd never told her he'd been a DEA agent either. They'd met in Montana, their relationship based on who they were at the time—not who they'd been. Or where they'd come from.

Maybe that had been the problem.

She looked over at him, shrugged. "I've been away from the village for so long."

He followed her around the next fallen spruce tree, and she made a sharp left. "Why did you leave the village?"

She shrugged again. "So few people, so few jobs, so much bullying. But mainly, smokejumping."

"Yes, I get that. Smokejumping was always in my blood too."

"Is that why you wanted to come to Alaska, to the Midnight Sun crew? To jump with your dad? I always thought you wanted Alaska for adventure."

"Yes, adventure, but . . . I miss him too." He ran his hand around the collar of his shirt. "Yeah." He pulled out his phone, tried Jade again, still no service. Slid the phone back in his pocket.

As they pushed their way to Ingriq, he spied a wild blueberry bush. He picked a couple, handed one to Cadee.

She grinned and popped it in her mouth.

Why hadn't she shared about growing up in this remote place back when they'd dated during smokejumping training?

Well, he had only told her about leaving California for adventure in Alaska with Midnight

Sun. They had become close by then, and it'd been the truth. But he'd been too concerned with his past.

He'd never explained the full "why" of going to Ember, pursuing wildland firefighting.

To anybody.

Too important to leave the old reputation back in California.

He pulled out his cell and tried to get Jade.

Nothing.

He slid it back in his Nomex pants pocket.

Almost smacked into Cadee because she stopped so quickly.

He stepped beside her. His breath caught as they stood gazing out over a half acre of fireweed, the gentle but tough pink flowers blooming from the pink stems. But only about a third of the way up, since it was June and the youngest flowers at the top had not yet opened. The flowers would bloom all the way to the top by September, the end of summer.

"I've never seen a fireweed meadow like this," he said. They weren't out of the forest. Spruce surrounded this fireweed.

She nodded. "I know, right?"

"No wonder you and your sister sneaked out here."

She smiled up at him. And again, the world shifted. Today, parting to uncover a window to the past when they'd had fun dating. *Race ya.*

Nope. Not now. He reached for his phone, took a picture for his mom, then followed Cadee across the meadow, pushing the flowers gently aside as he walked. He tried to step past, not on, the fireweed, some of it up to his ears. And he was six two. "This is a beautiful place, where you grew up."

She looked back, nodded. "It is beautiful."

For the first time in a good nine months, they were simply talking.

He'd been waiting... He ran his hands through his hair. "Cadee . . . can I ask you something?"

She turned to face him, her smile practically swallowing her face. "Of course."

"Never mind." He—he couldn't right now.

She tilted her head. "Okay. Listen."

He followed her example, and listened to the quiet of the forest for a long moment. "Listen to what?"

THREE

CADEE COULDN'T STOP HER GRIN. "So, can you hear the river?"

He grinned. "Of course. Must be near."

"Yep." She laughed. "I'll let you have the honors." She waved ahead at the last clump of fireweed.

Vince pushed his way through, and she followed him.

"This is a great river," he said. "So perfectly clear."

"Yep. This is the river Dad would take Emma and me to for fishing. If he got off work early." She knelt and filled her canteen. Sucked down water. Sometimes this part of Alaska was actually hot.

Vince knelt beside her and filled his own canteen. She wanted to tell him about Ingriq, but it seemed like her voice clogged with him around. Ever since his father had died.

Eventually she'd have to tell him exactly what had happened.

Then their business would be done.

Over.

She could take her broken heart and walk away from Vince Ramos forever.

She took out her ponytail, reset her elastic. Ingriq was a cool Alaskan place. Beautiful, of course. She'd liked Montana but didn't want to live anywhere but Alaska. And her Midnight Sun job sort of near Ingriq was perfect. She didn't want the fire to take its people, her people.

She scanned the sky. She didn't want to smile until she knew it was worth a smile. "Hey, Vince, are you seeing what I'm seeing?"

His head popped up to scan the sky with her. "Nice. Looks like the wind has shifted the fire from Ingriq and it's not as fast." He pulled out his Kestrel. "Windspeed is down, and it's headed east, not south. Away from your village. Humidity is even up a bit. It ought to be safe there."

They fist-bumped, but he looked into her eyes with a frown. The lines around his eyes softened. "Don't worry. We're still heading to Ingriq. Wind and humidity could change any moment."

She hadn't seen the soft facet of Vince in . . . well, a long while. It had been hiding behind those dark eyes, under the dark waves of his hair. "Yes. Any fire, anytime, could go crazy. But I'm not as uneasy as I was. For now. It's still too close." She pointed east, up the river. "Ingriq built a bridge down a distance. Maybe a two-minute walk from here. Wait till you see it. Jake Larson built it with his son, who was twelve at the time. It is architecturally awesome, I have to say."

He leaned down and filled his canteen with more water. Cadee did too. "With a twelve-year-old?"

Curiosity instead of silent anger? Another reminder of what used to draw her to him. "Yeah. Paul graduated from architecture school a couple years ago, being paid around the country for different projects."

"That's cool. You ready to go?" he asked.

"Ready." She slid her canteen into her gear bag and stood.

"Good. Let's head out." He headed downriver, and Cadee followed him.

He pulled out a baggie of orange slices as he walked. "Want some?"

"You and your fruit. You always have fruit."

"Or veggies. Health, you know."

Cadee laughed. "Of course I'll have some orange."

He tossed the baggie to her. She pulled out a couple orange slices and sped up to walk with him. She handed the bag back.

"I have a question," she said.

He popped an orange slice in his mouth. "Okay."

"That Kestrel. That was your dad's, wasn't it?"

"Of course you recognize it."

The burnt-orange handheld device had a silver wheel at the top, and under the small screen, it had arrows to choose what aspect of weather you needed to know.

She nodded, pointed at the scratch mark by the silver wheel.

He chuckled, spoke around the orange slice in his mouth. "'Who needs a weatherman?' Dad used to say. After he died . . ." He cleared his throat. "It was the only thing of his I kept."

She caught his glance, held it.

He blinked fast, and she put her hand on his shoulder. He stood there for a long moment, but something changed about his eyes. Something unsettling that she couldn't read.

His cell phone sounded, and he rubbed his

nose. He stepped away from her with a grin. "We're in cell service."

He pulled the phone out of his pocket, clicked it on speaker. "Hey, Jade. Cadee and I are here."

"Vince," came Jade's relieved voice. "You and Cadee all right?"

"Ran into some trouble, but so far it's been all right. Been trying to reach you. Everyone there okay?"

"I've been trying to reach you too. Took us a while to gather, but we're all good. Saxon got Neil out of the plane, but he's in bad shape. We just don't have Orion and Tori. Yet. Where are you?"

He looked over at Cadee, eyebrows raised.

Wow. Vince was looking to her for an answer. "We're at the Ingriq River," she said. "A couple miles from where we saw the plane smoke. Headed to Ingriq Village. I know a shortcut path from here. The fire's close to it." She glanced over at Vince. "I, uh, know my way around this area."

Jade said, "That's wonderful. I just now got a message. The wind keeps shifting."

Vince handed Cadee his phone, pulled out his Kestrel. Frowned at it. He looked back at her, nodded. Her stomach soured.

Jade continued. "The wildfire will track toward Ingriq Village, then suddenly turn. The hotshots are already en route to the village, but they'll need help. We'll try to meet you there."

Cadee leaned into the phone. "Are you sure the wildfire is staying away from the village, Chief?"

"Yes. Except, like I said, it does keep shifting. Get there as soon as you can, help them evacuate. I'm sending a warning to the trooper post."

"Copy that," Cadee said. "It's about an hour to the village. We'll follow Ingriq River." Her stomach grumbled, and she grimaced. She just hoped Jade couldn't hear it. "As long as none of those militia people on ATVs find us again, we'll be okay."

"ATVs? Were you shot at?"

"Yeah. No hits though," Vince said, moving the phone back to himself. "We hid until long after they were gone."

Jade huffed a breath. "Thank God. If you see them, keep running. That had to have been the militia. Law enforcement hasn't found all of those guys yet. I'm going to call Rio Parker, Skye's husband. He's local FBI, running point on the hunt for them. Be safe, both of you. Let me know when you get to the village. Later, you can both brief us on the militia."

"Copy that." Vince stowed his phone and his Kestrel in his pocket. Turned to Cadee, took a breath. "Cadee, why didn't you save my dad at the Aktuvik fire?"

Vince saw her tense.

Her eyes widened, her mouth opened, and she let out a gasp. "Vince Ramos, what on earth do you mean by that?"

He kept his voice even. "You were right there with Dad on the east spur of the fire. Why didn't you try to save him?"

Cadee swallowed. Turned away, kept walking. "Leave me alone," she whispered.

"What—are you kidding me?"

"I don't want to talk about it." She kept walking.

"Well, I do!" He didn't mean to thunder. He cut his voice down. "Cadee, I . . ."

"You really don't know?"

Vince stared at her. "What?"

"I loved your dad. He was . . . amazing. And everything. And . . ." Her eyes filled. "I can't believe you actually think . . ." She held up her hand. "Clearly, you don't know me at all."

"What do you mean? You were there!"

"So was the rest of the team—"

"But you were—we were . . ." He swallowed,

not sure he wanted to say the rest. "I thought we meant something to each other. I thought . . ."

She swiped her cheek, which was wet. Stared at him, her eyes fierce in his. "Yeah. Me too. Enough that you wouldn't for a second believe that I would abandon your father."

"Why not? You abandoned me."

Her mouth opened. She hurled words at him. "I abandoned you? You broke up with me right outside the church, right after Cap's funeral . . . your dad's funeral." Her voice softened. "You were grieving. I was grieving. I thought we'd be there for each other."

The grief almost drowned him. Again. He couldn't say anything.

Then her eyes grew hard as flint.

And his words forced their way out. "You abandoned my dad, so you abandoned me. Plain and simple."

Cadee's nostrils flared. She growled. "I. thought. we'd. be. there. for. each. other. But outside the church, *you* abandoned *me*." She crossed her arms, narrowed her eyes at him.

A buzz from his pocket. Not now.

It buzzed again, and he pulled it out.

A text from Tucker at the Midnight Sun admin office.

Tucker_____

Vince, I was glad to hear from
Jade that the crew is okay. But
I just got a phone news alert.
The DEA has a warrant for your
arrest. What's up?

He clicked on the link. Something about drugs and money laundering through real estate. He still had no clue.

But the DEA wanted to *arrest* him?

What on earth was going on?

Maybe the answer to his question didn't matter.

He looked over at Cadee.

Maybe he had bigger problems to solve.

FOUR

VINCE PLOWED DOWN THE PATH,
which was just barely flattened grass in spots.
Moose, Cadee presumed. Farther ahead, the
path would forge through salmonberry bushes.

She threw on her pack and followed Vince.

Slowly. She'd let him walk as far ahead as he
wanted.

You abandoned my dad, so you abandoned me.
How could he say such a thing? He knew Cap
had been like a dad to her.

What was Vince thinking?

*Okay, God. How could he even think I would
abandon Cap? How could he? God, we've got to be
teammates. Even if we can't be friends, we've got to
be teammates. How? How?*

Her fists unclenched. She took a deep breath.

It was grief. Nothing more. Grief had left him angry, dark. And it had left her . . . what? Racing into whatever fire she was fighting? Vince or no. Jade or no. Any of the Midnight Sun crew, it didn't matter. She just raced into a fire.

Sometimes she let loose on Vince. She bit her lips together. Sometimes she let loose on God.

Either one. Both.

Grief had left her bitter.

Forgive me, Jesus.

She stood still, her eyes closed.

No, she didn't feel forgiven. But forgiveness wasn't a feeling. Christ was at work in her life, and she'd just leave it at His feet.

Cadee opened her eyes. In the meantime, she needed to try to settle things with Vince. She jogged a bit and caught up to him where he was squatting by a birch tree, sipping from his canteen.

"Hey." She squatted beside him.

No response. Just that usual dark simmer.

She took out her canteen and had a drink. Stood and stowed it away.

Vince's brooding eyes stayed on the horizon. Why wouldn't he meet her gaze?

"Come on, Vince. Let's talk things out. We need to work together."

Still no response.

"We *must* be teammates and act as teammates. Look, I'm sorry I ran into the fire like I did at Resurrection Pass last month." Maybe that would lower the simmer? She did owe him an apology.

He stood. "Yeah. You did. I was shouting at you to stop, wait for the team's help. Not the only time, right? Well, congratulations on saving the woman. Is that what you need to hear?" He picked up his pack. "It's time to move out. Ingriq Village needs us. 'Bout time you showed up."

She heard an eagle's high whistle call as she and Vince stomped through salmonberry bushes and around spruce tree roots. But only silence emanated from Vince.

Suddenly, the smell of rotten fish attacked her nose. She drew to a stop. "I knew we were close to the river, but it doesn't usually smell this bad."

Vince tightly nodded his head. He shoved aside the last salmonberry clump and gestured her through.

She didn't want to go through, because she knew what they were about to see.

But she pushed past the bushes.

And there it was.

The river was clogged with fish bodies. It was a salmon die-off, the fish flowing with the river instead of swimming upstream to spawn. Mouths half open, they floated on their sides, shining with the fish oil in the water. Every now and then, there was a half-dead salmon, flopping weakly, trying to make it upstream. But it was clear it wouldn't.

"This is June. How is this happening?"

Vince barely held back the gag thanks to the smell of the dead salmon.

There were eddies where the bodies had gotten caught and spruce roots in the river that had caught some as well. Others were floating downriver. There was a relatively small cliff face on this side, but the other side of the river was flat, broad, with shallow spots that caught the fish too, until the current sped them on downriver.

It was a lot of dead salmon. There were hundreds—more, even, than after the annual spawning season.

Flies were heavy, and he waved his hand in front of his face to shoo them away.

He looked over at Cadee in her suspenders, her Nomex pants. Since their Ember training, he'd always seen that she was totally woman, totally firefighter.

No, they weren't going to be friends. But Jade

had forced—assigned—them to be partners. He popped his jaw back and forth.

He took a deep breath. He couldn't go down the forgiveness path. At least, not yet. But they did need to be teammates. He followed her to the edge of the cliff face. "This is crazy," he said. "It's salmon season. It isn't time for them to die."

"I've got my camera," she said. "I'm going to take a couple photos we can include in our debrief with Jade, because this is *not* normal."

Nothing about this was normal. Her response to his question about his dad, her outrage, really, when he was the one who should be furious.

Except, maybe he wasn't as furious as he initially had been. Not given her tears, her clear grief. So many secrets, and even more unanswered questions. But maybe they could wait.

"Let's get going. We need to get to Ingriq before the fire does," she said.

"Yeah, I saw the weather report Jade texted us. The wind there is almost as crazy as it was this morning, and it's supposed to get even crazier this afternoon. Let's just take a couple minutes."

Cadee nodded, and they separated, taking pictures as they walked along the cliff face.

Vince noticed a headband with stark red and black lines lying on the riverbank. He took a shot of it, along with the dead salmon. Probably it was nothing, but maybe it was something.

Suddenly, Cadee shouted, "Vince, come here!"

He took off running in her direction. Stilled.

She stood with a man who wore an almost blood-red Henley and black tactical pants—very military.

And clearly, the man had appeared out of no-where. Or had he been tracking them?

He was ruddy, blond, wearing a black wind jacket. The brashness of that—Vince would re-member this man, for sure.

Vince slowed, walked up. "Hey. What's up?"

"This is Landon." She offered a smile, but it seemed almost fake. Her eyes darted to the man, then back to Vince, holding his gaze. "Landon says he's Fish and Game."

He didn't believe the guy was from the Alaska Department of Fish and Game either. Vince stepped between them and dropped his fire pack on the ground next to Cadee's. He held out his hand to the guy. "Vince."

"What're you two doing out here?"

"We wanted to take a nice long hike on our lunch break." They were dressed in their smoke-jumper gear. What did the guy think they were doing? Vince forced a laugh. "Probably went too far off the road."

The man's eyes rose. "Yeah, you did."

"How about you?" Vince smiled. "What are you doing out here, Landon?"

"Boss wanted me to check out this river. The smell is terrible."

Vince turned, looked at the river, keeping the guy in his peripheral vision. The man was almost sending goosebumps up his spine. "This shouldn't happen during salmon season, right?"

"That's why it might not be safe for folks like you out here. Who knows what could happen?"

Vince's breath caught in his throat. Something about this guy was creepy. He wasn't sharing the truth with a creepy stranger. He wouldn't be surprised if this guy was one of those militia people who'd been chasing them, up to no good out here.

Was he responsible for the dead fish?

Landon also turned to the river. "This is a mess."

The guy had a gun in the back of his pants.

Vince pushed Cadee behind him. "It is. I've seen it, but not during a salmon season."

Landon seemed to frown, to consider the fish. "I certainly can't tell what's causing it."

A buzz came from his pocket, and he pulled

out his phone. He glanced at it, gave a forced sigh. "I gotta get back. Good luck on your hike. Hope you find a good salmon fishing spot."

Then the guy took off. At a run.

Vince and Cadee just stood there. Silently. She didn't step away as he expected her to. Instead, she threaded her arm through his.

"That was . . . weird."

"Let's get out of here."

In the distance, an ATV fired up. Headed away from them.

A few seconds later, Cadee whooshed out a breath. "He had a gun."

"Yeah. I saw it." And it had scared him to death.

Her eyebrows pinched together, and she massaged her neck. "But . . ." She shook her head. "After our argument . . ." She shook her head again. "So *that's* why you shoved me behind you."

"Of course. You think I'd leave you unprotected with a guy like that?" He frowned. "You think I'm gonna let you get hurt when I'm standing right here? With my DEA training—" He stopped himself, but it was too late.

"What?"

He bit his lips together, tight. Oops. Because now she'd ask why . . . and frankly, if he told her the truth, she would never look at him the same again.

Not that she looked at him the same now. But that was different.

She pointed at him. "No answer. Fine. But there is one thing I do deserve to know. Did you break up with me because of your dad?"

His throat tightened. But he nodded.

She closed her eyes, breathed deep. Squared her shoulders. "Right. Okay." She opened her eyes. "I sent Jade the pictures of the salmon. She can send them to Fish and Game. Let's get moving."

Right.

Cadee continued the trek to the village, but Vince needed a minute.

Forget her leaning up against him. Forget the way she'd threaded her arm through his.

They were apparently back to fighting.

Back to their stalemate.

More frustrated than he could handle, he walked up to the edge of the river and let his gaze slide over the salmon-packed river. There were hundreds of dead salmon. No way was this natural. Who had killed all these fish?

He glanced at Cadee walking away. Things between them hadn't gone at all like he'd hoped, deep in his heart.

Hoped? Oh, how had he gotten there? But maybe he had hoped for a different answer—any answer, really. Instead, he'd gotten accusations. Defensiveness.

Anger. As far as he could see, everything was falling apart. It was enough to make him—

The edge gave way. He slid down the steep, muddy incline. Snatched at a tree root sticking into the air. Missed. Grasped at a boulder. Missed. Splashed into the river.

Instead of a silted bottom, the riverbed dropped off into a strong current of icy snow runoff that caught the breath in his throat.

Stole it right out of him.

The flow of the river pushed his head beneath the surface. A salmon flowing down the river with him bumped into his head. Another hit his hand. Fish oil coated his hair, face, and hands as he struggled to keep above water.

Nomex pants might be great for fighting fire, but they were terrible for buoyancy. The water sucked him down. His boots dragged the bottom, and he kicked off.

He scraped at the water, batting it with both arms to force himself up for a breath. Finally, he pushed his head above the surface but shoved away a fish body from his face. He threw himself at a rock sticking up out of the water like an island.

He tried to grab the rock, but the fish oil slicked his hold, and he slid off. A logjam had caught a pool of dead salmon, and they pulled at his shirt. He pushed away from it, back into the current, and then he was swept downstream like a dead fish.

"Vince!" Cadee yelled.

He caught sight of her, running toward him along the cliff-face side, just before he got sucked under.

There was another rock poking out of the river. He threw himself at it.

FIVE

CADEE THREW DOWN HER PACK AND sprinted alongside the river. She jumped over a fallen spruce as Vince bounced up and down in the river's current.

He was about to come up to the waterfall.

The guy may have dumped her, and they certainly had their issues, but she wasn't going to let him die.

Like she hadn't let his father die, thank you.

Thank God. There he was, just up ahead. He'd caught hold of a rock sticking out of this side of the river. She sprinted up to the spot.

There—a brush shrub jutted most of the way down the cliff to the river. She lowered herself, inch by inch, and found good footholds. She pulled on the brush. It would hold her.

She hoped.

She let it take her weight. It did hold her. Thank God for the strong scrub brush.

Vince swept toward her. She reached down and held out her other hand. "Vince! Grab my hand!"

He reached up with his left hand, his other arm clinging to the rock.

She snagged his hand. It was slimy with fish oil, but she added her other hand. Braced her legs on the stone.

She pulled him close enough that he grabbed the cliff face. "Come on!"

He found a foothold. He let go of her and grabbed another handhold with his right. She backed away, ready to grab him if he needed help as he started climbing up the bank.

"You okay?"

He was gasping, his body flat against the wall of rocks. "Yes." He looked up at her. "Thank you. Let's get up this cliff." He got up and headed toward the edge.

Cadee let out a breath and turned to climb up after him.

The brush shrub she was holding on to cracked and snapped off, the dry vegetation coming away in her hand. No! Cadee's knee hit the ground, and she slid back toward the water. A scream wrenched itself from her lips.

Vince turned around. "Cadee!"

She grabbed for a handhold. Her fingers missed branches and rocks, scraping her hands.

She tumbled back and fell into the water.

Cold. Stinging. The river gulped her under, and she kicked hard, fighting for air. Surfaced.

Already, the current had yanked her a good five feet away. She beat at the water, tried for a regular swimming motion, fighting for the rocks. A dead salmon flowing down the current with her smacked her hand. The river's surge trapped her, dragged her downstream.

She went under, then surged back up, gasping.

She spotted Vince scrambling after her, shouting her name.

Wait. If she remembered right, there was a spot ahead where the bank on the other side was broad and flat. Before the waterfall. At that point, the river should slow down enough she could swim over to the edge. "Vince!"

A roar ahead.

The waterfall. The current sped up. No, no— she turned, kicking hard for shore.

The river crested over her.

With a scissor kick, she propelled herself to the surface.

The waterfall turned deafening.

She *wasn't* going to go down that waterfall and hit her head on a rock at the bottom. She still had fires to fight, life to live.

She kicked harder, her fingers dragging on a submerged rock.

The current sucked her down, and she was forced back underwater, but she kicked herself back up and gasped in another lifesaving breath of air.

But the river was winning.

Then, out of nowhere, a tree limb extended out in front of her. She grabbed it. Held on, even as her feet dragged under it, the river trying to unlatch her grip.

No.

A tug on the branch and she surfaced.

Vince! He stood at the bank, holding the end, reeling her in, so much intense concentration on his face that it galvanized her too.

She hoisted her torso onto the branch, which she tucked under her arm.

He kept reeling her in until she was close enough for him to lie on the bank and hold out his hand.

She let go of the branch, lunging to the hand-hold.

Cadee dangled by her left hand, smacking up against the rocky cliff. She bullied her right hand up and grabbed hold of stone. Feeling around with her feet, she located toeholds. For a moment, she just hung there. Just a moment.

"You can do this, Cadee!" Vince had both hands on hers now. "Climb!"

She worked herself up the cliff face. When Vince reached out for her and pulled her over the top, she flopped on her back, gasping, Vince lying down beside her.

Their puffs and pants were loud, about the only thing she could hear.

"You rock, Vince," she said between breaths.

"Gee, thanks."

Tears dripped down her face with the river water. Both of them could've died. She swiped the liquid away.

She tried not to laugh. But a giggle escaped.

And Vince started chuckling, an odd, rough sound that made her wonder when he'd last laughed.

"Oh, man," he gasped, one hand on his chest over his wet T-shirt. "I feel like a landed salmon trying to suck in air."

"Me too." She shivered, soaking wet and dripping from the river. Just like him. Cadee sat up and pinched her nose. "I smell like fish. Dead fish."

"And I'm slimy. Gross." He stood and offered her a hand to help her up. Good thing, because her legs wobbled.

"Thanks." She grabbed for his fingers, but their hands were so slimy she slid back to the ground. She shot him a silly glare and turned onto her side to push herself up.

And then she met his eyes, which had a spark in them—something of camaraderie, maybe even respect.

She knew that look. The kind he used to give her after one of their training sessions, when she'd impressed him. Or when they'd meet later at the Ember Hotline Saloon for a coke and a basket of fries and talk.

When they'd been friends, before they'd become more.

And now that her brain had gone there, she missed the warmth of his embrace in front of a movie. Oh, they'd been physically attracted to each other, for sure. Holding hands. Sharing a pizza at the Hotline or on base.

Even when she'd returned to Alaska and he'd

been in Montana, they'd stayed close with long video chats. They had even included Cap every now and then. Those two guys had cracked her up.

But then his father had died, and Vince had broken things off.

Those long conversations had been the glue of their relationship. They'd started at Ember long before all the hand holding and dates. And they'd been deep. Or funny. Or both.

Shoot. She missed him. And frankly, he did deserve answers.

The truth.

Her throat clogged with the thought.

Okay, then. Maybe.

Vince blew out a breath, nodded, as if reading her mind. "We better walk back and get our fire packs." He looked around. "We've ended up at least a mile *down* the river when we were headed upstream."

"Right."

They walked silently up the river, keeping a distance from the drop-off that had already tumbled them into the river once. The sun baked down on them, hopefully evaporating the smell and the slime of the fish.

Vince pointed to the side a couple feet ahead.

"There are our packs. I'll call Jade." He pulled his phone out of the pack's front pocket he'd stashed it in and punched away at it. "No signal." He slid his phone into his pants pocket on his shin.

They pulled on the fire packs. Overhead, the fire had grown, blackening the air. "How much farther?" he asked.

"Maybe a mile. Upriver this time."

He glanced at her, his mouth tugging up on one side. "Right."

They took off through the woods along the riverbank, winding around birch trees and spruce, then cutting onto a path toward the village.

She pulled and yanked at her Nomex pants and her shirt. They chafed.

"You okay?" He'd clearly caught her weird movements.

She nodded, but no. Not really. The urge to tell him sat like a ball in her chest. Worse, she'd known, ever since the accident, that God wanted her to tell Vince how his dad had died.

Courage, Cadee.

"Vince . . ."

He looked back at her.

"No one has told you the full story of your dad's death, right?"

"Of course not. Mainly you." He worked his

lips. "We were . . . we were getting serious. We *were* serious. *You* should have talked to me, told me what happened."

Yes. Yes, she should have. Her eyes teared up. "He was like a father to me. I was barely dealing with it."

He held aside a birch tree limb so it wouldn't smack her in the face. "Logan told me to ask you when I was ready to hear the full story about Dad."

"Are you?" she whispered.

"I am."

He's going to hate me even more, God. You have to help me!

She swallowed hard, glad she wouldn't see his face as they walked. "We were out on the east spur of the fire when the wind decided to change. We moved to get out of there." She blew out a breath. "Cap . . . there was a woman trying to save her dog—a Boston terrier. He saw her, began to run after her. Said that we should all move ahead. He'd be right behind us."

Vince frowned. "Dad shouldn't have done that."

She turned her head and caught his gaze. "Rule three. Base all actions on current and expected behavior of the fire."

"You don't have to quote the rule book to me."

"I'm just saying that your dad knew what he was doing. He followed the rules, Vince. We all did. We couldn't know that the wind would gust, change." She could feel the heat from that wind burning her skin now. She swiped a tear. "I mean . . . it . . . it raged. We saw it turn, saw it go after him—" She stopped, and a tear fell from her lid. "I tried to run in after him."

He'd turned, and now his mouth opened.

"Raine grabbed me. Practically had to pin me down. She kept saying, 'The fire's too big, Cadee.'" She looked away. "Even now, I keep hearing those words in my head."

He blinked. Hard.

"When Raine let go, I tried to run in again. This time, she got help from the others. They dragged me back, forced me to keep moving. I was a wreck—we all were."

Vince picked up a fallen spruce branch, snapped it in half, and lobbed the pieces into the woods.

Her voice was hoarse with the memory. "We found a safe place and tried to get to him. Black smoke was everywhere—it blinded us. We lost sight of him. And all I could hope was that he'd deployed his fire shelter."

Vince's mouth tightened. "Did he?"

"Of course. But it didn't … well, you know the rate of success on those."

He looked away, his eyes glistening.

Her voice fell. "Your dad did everything he could to save that woman." She took a step toward him. "We all did."

He closed his eyes. "That was so stupid, to run in after her—"

"No, it wasn't. She was trapped. Scared. You know how people get. They panic and stop thinking."

He nodded, opening his eyes. He kicked at the dead leaves and rocks. "Yeah."

"Your dad died a hero, Vince. I should have told you."

Vince nodded, gently grabbed her wrist. He turned in front of her. Face-to-face. Looking down at the forest litter at his feet, he took both of her hands in his.

Then he looked up. "There was nothing you could do."

She nodded, tears streaming down her face. "There was nothing I could do."

"I see now why everyone has been prompting me to ask you to tell me the story." He let go of her hand. "I guess we both needed to hear that."

Oh.

Yes.

She stilled, even as he turned and headed out ahead of her on the trail.

Vince probably needed some time to process what'd happened with his dad.

Probably?

Certainly.

She walked slowly behind him.

A few minutes later, he paused, let her catch up to him.

One corner of his mouth rose. "Thank you for trying to save my dad."

"Of course. Like I said, your dad was—he was like a father to me."

His jaw worked. "I've been so angry, I just never asked how it happened." He moved closer, pulled her into the warmth of his arms. Then he looked into her eyes, bit his lower lip. Like he used to when they were going to kiss.

She tingled all over. She smoothed her ponytail behind her shoulder.

He leaned down.

Crack!

A gunshot! Cadee stiffened.

Crack!

"Run!" Vince grabbed her hand and didn't let go as he took off through the woods.

Wow, these people were persistent.

He pulled her off the trail, toward the salmonberry bushes. They dove under the first bush and crawled deep into the massive stand, getting poked by thorns and scraped by the branches. Then he tucked her in tight. "Don't move."

And frankly, he didn't mind having her to hold on to—just for a moment, her story thick in his mind, even as he listened for footsteps.

She'd tried—really tried—to save his dad. And he was a jerk for believing otherwise for so long.

It hadn't been completely his fault. When the guys had told him to ask Cadee, and when she'd gone radio silent on him, he'd let a lie sit in his gut.

Grow.

"Do you hear them?" She lay in his arms now, her back to his front, gripping his backpack straps. She smelled like the river, but he'd forgotten how dangerously perfect she felt in his arms.

He didn't dare move to brush off the bumblebee that landed on her shoulder, but thankfully, it was distracted by the berries.

At least the breeze was strong enough to rustle

the leaves of the heavily covered bushes so the gunmen wouldn't be able to tell where they were.

He hoped.

"Yes." And now he could see their boots, stomping up and down the edge of the bushes. Looking for them.

Was this more militia? How—

And then he got it. Landon.

So, not with Fish and Game.

"Don't breathe," he said into her ear.

They lay quietly, unmoving, until the ATV engines kicked to life in the distance.

Cadee pushed herself up off the ground.

"Stay down." Vince tugged on her pack and she dropped beside him.

She looked exhausted. He certainly was.

Spruce cones dug into his thigh, but he kept his head low.

And then a dog raced through the brush, barking and snarling. Another joined in, so there were at least two.

So they weren't done.

The snarls grew louder as the animals came nearer.

A man yelled, "Gunner! Cobra! Come look over here!"

The man whistled and the dogs ran off.

Cadee's hand tightened around Vince's. They lay still, hand in hand, a team.

Felt a little like them before his dad's death.

Of course his dad had tried to save a woman in trouble. And of course the wildfire had done its own angry thing.

Maybe he'd even pray. Tell God how he felt about what'd happened to Dad.

Later.

Right now, he'd just stay hidden with Cadee.

He remembered a time during training when they'd both gotten in trouble for laughing— they'd been sent on a five-mile, uphill run with hundred-pound packs—when the training camp leader had shouted "giddyup" at the team as they climbed ladders.

That was when the conversations between them had really started. Coffee or running or weightlifting. Conversations that'd gotten deep, that'd made him fall in love with her. Then there'd been the movie they'd run out of, laughing way too loudly. The popcorn kid had just stared at them.

Cadee had once gotten all indignant when he'd beaten her at bowling. And then she'd made fun of him for really thinking she'd been mad at him. He thought about the times in his college years that Dad had stepped in, teaching him how to adult. And when they included him during their Montana-Alaska video chats with him, he'd seen his old man act like a father to Cadee. He loved that. The piece of his father that they shared.

Yeah. They'd been getting serious.

Until he'd broken it off. Because he'd believed a lie that he'd made up in his head.

A branch cracked.

Vince ducked his head back down.

Was this one of the gunmen who'd chased their plane, the ones Jade had said were most likely militia? The feet stomped close to them, and Vince held his breath. It could be the people who'd chased them yesterday or the guy they'd met at the river.

He waited a couple of seconds and then lifted his head, just barely. Enough to recognize him. Landon, the guy from the salmon die-off. He could practically guarantee the guy was militia too. He still had a gun.

The man walked the opposite direction, toward the dog guy.

Vince gently shifted so he could look at Cadee. *Shh*, he signaled.

Her lips were pinched tight. She didn't need

the signal. He squeezed her hand, and she gave him a small smile.

"Boss has been waiting long enough," Landon grumbled. "They must have run on ahead. You guys go; I'll stick around and find them. They'll be dead by nightfall."

In his arms, Cadee stiffened.

And he made a vow to himself, right then, to keep her alive.

Vince and Cadee lay silently for five minutes after Landon's stomps had finally faded into the distance. They waited a few more minutes, and he heard a truck and an ATV fire up and the gunmen drive off.

Vince let out a breath. "I think we're clear."

Cadee coughed as they sat up, wiped the dirt away from her mouth. "What do these guys want?"

"No idea. But I'm not sticking around to ask. Let's go." They took off, running now. "How much farther?"

"Just beyond—"

An ATV engine, too close.

He grabbed her pack and directed her behind a large boulder. Vince peeked around it. Same ATV. Landon. Again. Keeping his promise to continue looking for them.

Cadee scooted closer to him, shoulder to shoulder. They froze, stock still. He barely breathed. Met her eyes.

They were so blue. Terribly, perfectly blue.

And despite the crazy, dangerous moment, all he could think of was how she used to kiss him. How she might kiss him again.

The ATV took off slowly in the direction they were headed. Toward Ingriq.

But neither of them moved. Her shoulder sent a wave of warmth into his. She looked up at him, her mouth parting.

Wait—was she thinking the same thing? He touched her cheek.

She brushed off dead leaves stuck to his shirt.

"I've been thinking," she said. "Look at where that man headed. My *family*'s in Ingriq. My *friends*. He's hunting for us now. We can't let that creep get to the village before us."

His eyebrows rose.

She shrugged like it was an easy task. "Turn the tables so he doesn't hurt an innocent because of us. I know a shortcut. We can beat him there."

Vince gave a long, slow nod. "Warn the village. Maybe even arm ourselves."

"Let's move." She took off, running up the path.

He pulled out his phone and sent Jade a quick message.

Then he clicked to take another look at the message that had his stomach all clenched.

From Tucker.

Tucker_____
ETA? Just had DEA in my office.

Cadee led them through the woods full of moss and spruce roots to climb over.

A bright orange mushroom growing halfway up the trunk of a spruce tree caught his eye, and he nearly smashed into Cadee, who'd stopped suddenly.

She looked at her watch. "This is the path leading to the road I told you about. Landon will be here any minute," she said under her breath.

The dirt path led to their left and to their right. He looked both ways. "How do you know he isn't already past us, Cadee?"

She rolled her eyes. "Shortcut, dude."

"Let's go," he said, but she put a hand on his arm.

"Wait. What if we try and take him out before he gets there? One of us goes across the path, down about twenty yards. Me." She pointed left. Then she pointed right. "And you about five yards that way. And we flank him. Knock him out, grab his gun when he gets halfway between us on the path."

"Wait—what?"

"We can do this."

She was serious.

"No. No *we*. Good idea, but I will take him down."

She spread her arms akimbo. "You don't need to protect me."

He rounded on her. "This isn't like your self-defense class, Cadee. This guy has a gun. I'm trained for situations like this. I don't want you shot."

She nodded slowly, like he was figuring things out. "I don't want *you* shot."

He rubbed at his temple.

"I only have a self-defense class, but I can at least help, Vince."

"How?"

"I'll distract him. You jump him."

He stared at her, seeing it, still not liking it. But . . .

It could work. "Fine. But when I say get down, you get down."

Her mouth tightened, but she nodded.

They fist-bumped, and Cadee jogged down a short distance to the left. Once she was hidden across the path, he turned and jogged about twenty yards down to a spot on his side. He dropped his pack to the ground and scrunched into the V formed by two close spruce. He squatted down where their roots kind of formed a nest and he could see clearly down the path. Hidden.

His eyes narrowed. He was going after Landon's legs. *Okay, God? Never mind. I'm doing this regardless what You say. Just keep Cadee safe.*

Maybe he'd have a real talk with God later.

Until then, he would see if God showed up to help.

He heard the sound of boots on the path, headed this way.

Landon.

He shifted to see down the path toward Cadee and squatted back down. Vince watched as militia guy walked past him a couple feet.

And then Cadee.

She stood up, as if not seeing Landon, and bam!

Now!

Vince leaped out, launched to tackle the guy, and grabbed his legs.

Landon fell face down into the dirt, then turned and slammed his fist into Vince's ear.

His ears rang. Loudly. Dazed him. Landon

scrambled out of his grip. Kicked him in the chest and sent Vince windmilling back.

Cadee sprinted down the road. She kicked Landon's fallen gun off the path and into the woods.

Landon jumped to his feet, facing her. Breathing hard. Cadee looked ready to fight him, of course, but Vince could use this. Landon was so focused on her—

Vince jumped on Landon's back. Landon spun, knocking Vince to the ground, and leaped toward Cadee. But Vince had fallen just right to grab Landon's feet. Again. He grasped both boots and pulled back, not even caring if he got kicked again.

Landon toppled back to the ground. Cadee pounced on him and pulled back his arms.

Breathing hard, Vince sent a knee into the man's shoulder. Nice to know his DEA training was useful. He grabbed a zip tie out of the pocket at the bottom of his pants and restrained Landon.

Cadee rolled off Landon's back, also breathing hard. Vince pulled the man up.

Then Cadee stood, jogged into the woods, and a minute later came back bearing the man's gun.

Vince's jaw dropped. "Good job keeping track of where you kicked that thing."

She handed him the gun and swiped at the dirt on her pants and shirt. When she was done, she jerked her head at Landon. "Guess who's coming to the village with us."

The guy's lips became a straight line.

Vince shook his head. "You will not be shooting at us anymore, dude."

Vince and Cadee fist-bumped. Then Vince grinned, pushed militia guy ahead of him and behind Cadee, who led them toward Ingriq.

So yeah, maybe God had shown up to help them. Vince might actually have to admit Cadee was right about that.

SIX

FINALLY, SOMETHING THAT SEEMED like a win.

It had been long enough. After running for their lives, both of them taking a dip in the river, and then more gunmen—and attack dogs—Cadee now felt better than she had in days.

They were finally headed to Ingriq, and they had one of the bad guys tied up, headed for custody.

"Let me guess, you two are going to leave me zip-tied to die in the wildfire at Ingriq," Landon sneered, walking between Cadee and Vince in single file as they stopped at the paved road in front of them, Ingriq one way, Copper Mountain the other. Finally, they were done with the faint shortcut path and out of the backcountry.

She lifted her eyes to the heavens. "Leaving people for dead is not what they pay us for."

Vince snorted, winked at her.

She grinned. They had so many wins, working together and saving each other. And she'd told him how his father had died. Letting go of the guilt and pain was a win too.

And now he was coming to her home.

"Wait till you see the village, Vince," she said. "It's like each house is cozied into the woods. Some families are poor, but all are close enough together to support and love each other."

"Is it an Alaskan Mayberry?" he said.

Landon snorted.

Except for that mean girl back in high school. She bit the inside of her cheek for a second. "Mostly." She tilted her head at Landon. "My ex is an Alaska State Trooper. Jared Jensen. Let's take Landon to Jared's house. It's right up ahead, just outside of Ingriq. Bet he's still there, helping people now that Jade made sure a warning was issued. But if not . . ." She shrugged.

"If not, he'll stay in my custody while we help with evacs." Vince put his hand on Landon's shoulder to prevent him from running. "So, how far from Ingriq are we, Cadee?"

She grinned, motioned to her left and her

right. "Copper Mountain to the west is about nine miles away. Ingriq is about a ten-minute walk from here."

One corner of his mouth rose as he read aloud the sign pointing to Ingriq. "State maintenance ends here. Drive at your own risk." Vince gave a bark of laughter. "Alaska Mayberry, here we come."

She chuckled and led the way down the pot-holed dirt road decorated with spruce. The people in this cozy little town loved this place, potholes and all—they didn't want to be part of "big city" Copper Mountain with all of a thousand people. And forget Anchorage. Besides, this was an Alaska-beautiful place. Aunt Claire knew the owner of the Corner Store, and that connection was how Dad got the garbageman job. He'd *needed* a job. It wasn't great, but she and Emma had come to love the place.

A few minutes later, Cadee noticed a burgundy car parked up ahead at the side of the road, a faded bumper sticker on the trunk. *I make asthma look good.* Emma had put that on her car to bring a smile to Ava's face.

No. Cadee bolted to the car and looked into the windows.

Blast! There was the plug-in oxygen concentrator sitting right there in the back seat with two suitcases and a box of granola bars.

Why was the car headed *into* town? This made no sense.

Vince stopped next to her. "Wow. That car's tire sure got shredded."

"This is Emma's car." Cadee looked around, expecting them to appear anytime. "Where is she? And Ava."

Vince tried to open the doors. Locked. She'd been so panicked she hadn't even thought of that.

A rock on the side of the road would do the trick. Cadee ran over for it and cocked her arm back.

"What are you doing?" Vince said, his grip on Landon.

"That's Ava's oxygen concentrator." Then she threw the rock at the driver's window. It shattered. She reached in and hit the unlock button.

Cadee opened the back door and grabbed the concentrator.

"Emma would never, never leave the concentrator behind. Especially not with a wildfire threatening her daughter's ability to breathe."

"Cadee, we don't know where she actually is. They might've been picked up."

She narrowed her eyes at him. They hadn't

been quick enough getting here. Now her family was at risk, and they still needed to deliver Landon to Jared.

"You know the rules like I do. Be alert. Keep calm."

Standard Firefighting Order number six was engraved on her brain tissue. "Think clearly. Act decisively."

He tilted his head. "Not frantically."

Yeah, frantically was not a standard order. She felt her heart calm just being here with him. Vince was right.

He grabbed the zip tie holding Landon's hands behind his back, and they kept walking.

They made the big curve before the village. It wouldn't be long before the dirt road with more potholes than road would appear. And Ingriq's houses—some newly painted, some peeling—and trailers.

And up ahead . . .

"It's Emma." Her sister carried Ava on her back and a suitcase in each hand. They had matching swinging blonde ponytails, matching bright-red scrunchies, and matching lime-green T-shirts. Emma trudged slowly along the blacktop, headed back to town. After a failed attempt to escape the coming fire storm? Cadee stopped in her tracks, nearly stumbling at the sight of them.

Alive.

"Go. We're behind you," Vince urged from behind her with Landon.

Emotion always made her voice catch. She mouthed *Thanks* and handed him the concentrator.

She sprinted down the road. "Emma!"

Her sister dropped the suitcases and slid Ava to the ground. She whirled around, her wide-legged yoga pants throwing up dust, and came running.

"Oh, Cadee. Thank God. I . . ." Then tears started to fall—sobs.

Tears trickled down Cadee's cheeks too. She reached her sister and grabbed her in a strong hug.

"We didn't expect you," Emma whispered. "But we need you. I was trying to get Ava out of the way of the smoke, but . . ."

"The flat tire. I know."

"I couldn't carry the luggage and the oxygen concentrator. I was hoping for a car to pass by, but . . ."

"I know. Vince and I are here."

Ava tugged at Cadee's sleeve, her ponytail bouncing up and down. The women's emotional roller coaster swooped from tears to chuckles.

Cadee reached down, grabbed Ava up, and spun her around. Her long lime-green T-shirt whirled around over her black leggings. "Sorry I missed your birthday party, Miss Seven-Year-Old."

"It was fun." Ava giggled. She showed Cadee a sparkly bracelet on her wrist. "See what Jenny gave me?" She coughed.

Emma whooshed out a nervous breath, and Cadee felt her nerves clench up her stomach. "That is beautiful," Cadee told her niece. "How are you, Ava? Are you okay? I saw your car."

"I'm okay, sort of, but the car has a messed-up tire," Ava said.

"Messed-up tire for certain. But I'm glad you're okay." Cadee squeezed Ava. Gently. Caught Emma's gaze over Little Miss's head. "Why on earth were you headed *into* town?"

Emma turned a little pink. "We thought we'd forgotten her inhaler. I turned around to go back and get it, and that's when Ava found it, and then the tire got shredded. We're headed back to Corner Store, where a couple buses from Wasilla are picking up wildfire evacuees, thanks to Aunt Claire."

Cadee smiled. "Of course she organized that." But the situation curbed her smile. "That wildfire is still trying to decide whether or not to head into Ingriq. Smart to head out."

Emma rubbed Ava's shoulder.

Cadee turned to see Vince and Landon walking up.

"Oh my goodness!" Emma squealed. "You got her concentrator! I'm so thankful." She glanced between Cadee and Vince. "Wait. Is this *Vince*? *The* Vince?"

Ava jumped up and down, wildly waving at him. "Hi! I'm Ava! I'm seven. My birthday is in April. When is your birthday? I live in Ingriq. Where do you live?"

Chuckling, Vince squatted down. "Hi. I'm Vince. My birthday is in January. I live in Copper River."

"What's your favorite toy? Mine is my Jewel Dragon. Her best friend is Gem Dragon."

Emma squatted down. "Hey, why don't you get Jewel Dragon out of your backpack and play over in the grass while we talk?"

Ava giggled. "Yeah." But she stopped and pointed at Landon. "Who's the guy with the broken hands, Aunt Cadee?"

Cadee choked back a laugh. "His hands are okay. We're just keeping him safe. He is Mr. L."

And that was all she'd say, rather than give Ava the name of a criminal.

Landon rolled his eyes.

"Oh, okay." Ava plopped in the grass with her backpack and dug around for her toy.

Vince stood, glanced at Cadee, then her sister. "It's nice to meet you. Emma, right?"

She nodded, a knowing smile on her face. They shook hands.

Cadee closed her eyes for a moment. She'd be getting a text from her sister to discuss Vince. "Anyway, Vince, let's help Emma get Ava and the suitcases to Corner Store. We can stop at Jared's house on the way."

Emma's eyebrows waggled. "You wanna see Jared, huh?"

Vince's eyes went wide in response to Emma's tease. Ridiculous.

"He'll take care of Mr. L."

Emma cringed. "Oh."

Vince snorted, turned to Emma. "I've got Mr. L. and the concentrator."

Cadee gave Ava a wink, motioned her over. "I've got my favorite little girl," she said and swung her onto her back. With the action-figure dragon.

"I've got her backpack and the suitcase," Emma said.

They headed down the road to Jared's house, just outside of Ingriq proper. Basically a one-room log cabin. His nice boat sat in his driveway with his nice SUV. Just like when they were dating. He was a solid guy, a for-real church guy. A hot guy, with intense gray eyes, a perfectly trimmed mustache and beard, and a bald head. But their lives hadn't been heading in the same direction.

Obviously.

Jared had wanted a woman who would stick around. Not one who flew all over, jumping out of planes to fight fire.

Then she'd met Vince, who'd understood the wild, untamed thing inside her. Because his heart beat to the same rhythm.

When they got to the house, she walked up and knocked on the door, hoping Jared wasn't gone, running around town helping people.

He opened the door, mid bite of the sandwich in his hand. "Cadee!" He wiped the crumbs off his mouth. "What a surprise. Glad I stopped in for some food, since you showed up." He set down the sandwich on the shoe bench right inside his door, wiped his hands on his AST shirt, and ran his hands through the stubble on his chin. He then caught sight of her sister. "Hi, Emma. Hi,

Ava," he called. He waved at them and stepped outside.

Froze for a second.

His voice dropped to almost inaudible, and he pivoted, pulled back his denim jacket so Landon could see his gun but Ava couldn't. "What are you doing with Landon Russo, Cadee?"

She dropped Ava down. "Go see if your mama has a granola bar or something, okay?" Ava ran over, and Emma walked her to the top of the driveway, where they'd left their suitcases and the fire packs she and Vince were carrying.

Jared crossed his arms and just stood there.

"He tried to kill us. Shot at us, twice. We flanked him, took him out."

Jared cleared his throat, jerked his head toward Vince.

Oh yeah. "Jared, this is my co-firefighter Vince Ramos. Vince, this is Trooper Jared Jensen."

Jared turned, waving backward as he jogged to his SUV and pulled a pair of handcuffs out of the console. He jogged back and switched out the zip tie for the cuffs. "We've been looking for this guy for a couple months. I'll drive him into the Copper Mountain lockup for a formal arrest."

He held Landon's head as he pressed him into the back seat of the SUV.

"I have rights," Landon shouted.

Jared closed the door. A little hard. Cadee grinned. Just like Jared.

He turned to Vince and reached out his hand. "Hello, Vince."

Well, this was awkward.

Vince reached out to shake the trooper's hand, something tightening in his gut. Cadee had turned a little red.

As if embarrassed? Why?

Jensen shook his hand. "I'm Jensen, AST."

"Ramos, former DEA."

Jensen tipped his chin in the air. "Pleasure. We've needed this guy for a long while. We'll add attempted murder to his drug and militia charges." He pointed at Vince's Nomex pants. "That his gun?"

Oh. Of course. "Yes." Vince pulled it out of his front pants pocket and held it out to the trooper so he could enter it into evidence.

Cadee wore a strange, tight smile.

Jensen stuck it in the back of his pants, then stuck out his hand toward Vince. "Thank you."

Vince nodded. "Thank you, Jensen."

"Call me Jared."

Gone were the days where, as a Fed, he'd dealt with local law enforcement. Now Vince had to wonder, was this guy being nice to him because Vince was a firefighter . . . or because he was with Cadee? He had to admit, Jared seemed like a decent guy—someone Cadee would love to build a life within the community she loved.

But then he thought about her smile around Midnight Sun. Yeah. She wouldn't be happy staying home. She was too happy firefighting.

"I'm Vince." He chuckled at himself. He'd been trying to impress with the whole former-DEA thing. "Smokejumper now."

Jared smiled. "What're you two doing up in Ingriq?"

"Fire and evacuation assessment."

"I hoped you'd say that. The warning went out a couple hours ago. Some have left in their own vehicles. Others are meeting the bus at Corner Store. I'm guessing the bus will need to take two trips to get everyone out of there." Jared glanced at Vince, then back at Cadee. Under his breath, he said, "The gray house needs help."

Cadee winced.

Jared simply nodded.

Vince took a look at the smoke billowing up from the Ingriq fire as the wind whipped through

VONI HARRIS

the valley, flinging debris in the air. "Can't guarantee there's time for anyone to make two evacuation trips to Copper Mountain. The wind is shifting from this morning."

Jared nodded. "I'll let people know to pick up their pace. We don't have long."

Was this guy going to be the last one out of town, like a captain going down with his ship? Vince tapped his toe inside his boot, waiting for further discussion about this gray house, but there was none. Not from Jared or Cadee.

He'd have to ask straight out. Vince crossed his arms, looking at Jared. "We can hit all the houses to check evacuation, but what is this 'gray house?'"

Jared narrowed his eyes at him, then looked to Cadee.

"Jared, this is Vince Ramos, as in the son of Captain Ramos."

"Oh. I've heard of the captain." He looked at Vince. "I'm sorry for your loss."

"Thanks." Vince swallowed against the lump in his throat.

Cadee said, "Vince is a solid guy like his father."

And still, neither of them answered his question about the house.

Jared stepped toward Cadee. "I didn't know

you were still with Midnight Sun. You haven't messaged me in a while."

She stared at the ground.

"Do you still have my number, or did you conveniently lose it?" The edge of a smile curled up Jared's lips.

Vince didn't really want to be standing here for this.

She looked up at the trooper, smiling. "Of course I still have it."

Right. Vince was out of here. "We should get to work."

"Please text me when Ingriq is empty." Jared jerked his head toward Landon. "I have to get him to Copper Mountain, of course. But since the two of you are here . . ."

"I'll let you know how the evac goes. And I'll tell Vince about the gray house after we've gotten Emma and Ava to the Corner Store to catch the bus."

Jared gave Cadee an awkward hug, waved at Vince, and jumped into the SUV with the Alaska State Trooper decal on the side.

"Let's go." Cadee headed out.

Vince watched her ponytail wave back and forth as she headed up the driveway to where

Emma and Ava were playing. Yeah, he'd talk to Cadee about the ex later.

Maybe she'd left a trail of broken hearts all across Alaska, and he'd never known.

He followed her, and they grabbed the two suitcases. Ava started to jump on Emma's back, but Emma gave her the duck face, rubbed her back. "No, ma'am. I've carried you a lot of the way so far. It's only, like, a three-minute walk from here, and you've got the inhaler in your pocket. Let me know if you need to jump on my back, but only if you *need* to."

Pouting, Ava flopped to the ground.

Emma's eyebrows rose. "Ava . . ."

Ava giggled, stood up, and started skipping down the road into town.

Emma shook her head with a grin. "It's more like five minutes, but don't tell her that."

Vince picked up the small suitcase and the concentrator. Cadee gave her sister a side hug, picked up the other suitcase, and they walked single file down the road behind Ava.

They entered the city from the west and found the Corner Store easily: log-cabin style, next to another log cabin—a local art center. A plant store, and an after-school-program building looked the same except for their signs. Denali and

Copper Mountain made a gorgeous background to the cozy city home and the forest they'd walked through.

No wonder Cadee had been so determined to join the Midnight Sun crew as soon as she was done with smokejumper training. That way she could stay close to home. That and her obvious heart for her family. She'd gone to Ember because, by reputation, it was the most challenging training course in the nation. Vince had been there for the same reason.

To get ready for Midnight Sun.

Vince looked at his watch. "Four minutes."

"Thanks for the help," Emma said, and crushed him into a hug. "I don't know what we would've done if you hadn't found us." Then she gave Cadee a long hug.

Ava took a leap, flying into Vince's arms, landing on his fire pack like a chair. She circled her arms around him.

Startled, he chuckled and swung her around.

If he hadn't broken up with Cadee, this adorable kid would've been in his life by now—in more than just the bare-bones stories Cadee had told him about her family.

A gentleman wearing a wide-brim blue baseball cap that matched his sky-blue eyes came jogging out of the store, followed by a teen couple holding hands, a family of four, and an older gent. The man was apparently the owner, since he matched the logo on the sign. "Emma," he called. "You and Ava riding the bus? It'll be here in about two minutes. We're lining up by the gas pump."

Ava slid down like it was a big adventure. "Yay!"

They all said their goodbyes as Emma and Ava walked in, the store owner carrying their suitcases for them. Man, they'd still have been on their way to Corner Store if Emma'd had to carry all of that herself. And they wouldn't have the concentrator. Ava coughed as she waved at him and Cadee. Emma nudged her, and she pulled out her inhaler.

He waved back. "What's up with Ava's dad?" His eyes were drawn to the smoke in the sky.

"It was a divorce situation that Emma didn't want but couldn't help," she said, eyes on the sky.

"Mm. Rough," Vince said, looking at the trees to judge wind speed and direction. Time was breathing heat down their necks. He emptied his water bottle, wiped his mouth with his sleeve. "This is the main road?"

Cadee chuckled. "Mostly. The gray house, with the rose bushes beneath the window two houses down?"

He nodded.

"It's a safe house for abused women," she said under her breath.

Oh. "How do you know that?"

"A friend of mine. That's all I have to say. Hang back a bit, but we need to go in there together. Several of the women might need help."

No wonder Jared had worried about him finding out the location of a safe house. "And I'm male."

"But it will take two of us to help. So yes, you are male, but you are trustworthy, solid, steady, gentle, sensitive . . ."

He didn't know what to do with her words or the way they landed in soft soil. And the trust in her relentless, fearless blue eyes turned him mute.

". . . pigheaded, irritating, argumentative."

Oh. Well.

Her stoic expression split into a grin. Cadee slapped his shoulder. "I wouldn't want to over-inflate your ego."

Vince shook his head, started to say something, but then he spotted a guy down the street waving his hands and jogging in their direction.

Instinct had him dropping the suitcases by the vehicle and moving to intercept the man. When he got close enough, he stilled.

What was Nick Atwood doing here?

In a rush, years of his life flooded back into his mind, like falling into that river, being swept away by a current so much stronger than him.

Nick Atwood, his colleague for three years. A fellow DEA special agent.

Here.

On a day when Vince had found out there was a warrant out for his arrest? Yeah, right, it was a coincidence.

Nick still looked all DEA with deliberately messy hair and a scruffy face, jeans, and his eyes roving around.

Vince didn't want to introduce him to Cadee, because he needed to find out what was up. He turned to Cadee. "I'll meet you out in front of the gray house in five minutes."

She gave him a weird look but jogged toward the first house on the left side of the road.

Nick crossed the street. "Hey, Vince! I thought that was you. How are you, Mr. Midnight Sun?"

They gave each other a quick hug, thumping each other's backs.

"Wow, man, you stink. Have you been swimming with fish?"

Vince laughed. "Long story, but I bet my boss will hose me off at the jump base. Crazy running into you up here. Were you trying to find me?"

It was some kind of coincidence, his former partner finding him up here.

Nick shoved Vince's shoulder. "Figures you'd be in trouble out here and need my help."

Vince snorted. "I'll have you know, Cadee and I arrested a bad guy earlier."

"Cadee?"

"My colleague." Why was he twitchy about introducing her to his former California DEA partner? He was the man who—after all of the DEA's suspicion and chaos—advised him to go into firefighting. Alaska for adventure. The Midnight Sun with Dad. It was the best advice.

He hadn't told Cadee anything about his DEA past—only that he'd been an agent for a few years. It wasn't as if he'd wanted to admit he'd walked away under a cloud of suspicion.

At least Nick had believed Vince had nothing to do with it. Vince had never been a dirty Fed.

His friend said, "I'm up here on a last-minute real-estate business trip, thought I'd see you while I'm here. Your boss said you were in Ingriq, so I came up here to catch you."

Vince couldn't help but grin. This larger-than-life guy was a friend—more than just a partner. Vince said, "So, how's your new job?"

Nick huffed a laugh. "You know me. I couldn't

totally give up my connection to the DEA, so I'm still doing contract work. But I'm loving it. Making money."

Vince tapped his shoulder. "How's your wife?"

His face softened. "You should see what she's done to our landscaping. A huge greenhouse."

"Nice."

"Yeah. She's turning it into a garden business."

"Of course. What a perfect way to add to your beautiful house." An expensive house. For a DEA agent. Something that had never quite seemed to jive for Vince. Not that he'd ever have said anything about it, given the accusations flying around the DEA at the time. Everyone had been under suspicion. Which meant they'd had no idea who was dirty.

But Nick had never given Vince reason to doubt his integrity.

The wind sent a gust down the street, blowing more smoke into the area.

"Listen, it's real good to see you, but this isn't a safe area. There's a wildfire up here. Cadee and I are here to assess the fire and the process of evacuation. You need to evacuate with the rest of these people."

Nick laughed. "I know, I know. I heard about it when I got to Ingriq. Was just getting ready to leave when I saw you, Mr. Fire Hero." He thumped Vince's back. "Maybe we can talk more later."

One corner of his mouth rose. Nick was always a tease. Made partnering with him both fun and successful. "Yeah. Hope so, partner."

Nick chuckled and ran toward his sedan a couple blocks away.

"Hey, one sec, Nick!" Vince jogged to his friend. "Do you know anything about the DEA having a warrant out for my arrest?"

Nick shook his head. "I haven't heard anything about it."

"Okay." Vince stepped back, more than a little disappointed he still didn't have answers. "Thanks, bro."

Nick gave a backward wave as he ran to his car.

If Nick knew nothing about the warrant, then the situation couldn't be that bad. Right?

The wildfire caught his eye, the blaze lighting the sky above the spruce trees. The smoke was thick like pea soup fog.

Whoa. It had grown.

He looked at his Kestrel. The fire had created its own weather, and the crazy wind they'd landed in yesterday had suddenly gone crazier. It was headed this way. Fast.

He looked over at Cadee, who had noticed it as well. Their gazes met, and he gave her a brief nod.

She came over. "We've got to get the gray house ladies out of here."

"Yep."

They walked up the rock path to the door. Cadee knocked.

A big-haired woman, about their age, opened the door. Behind her, the place was chaotic with eight women trying to make phone calls, pack suitcases, make sandwiches—obviously trying to prepare to leave. In a sort of organized panic.

"Mackenzie!" Cadee said. "I heard you became director here. How exciting. Our school did its best by you."

"You too, Cadee!" Mackenzie clasped her into a hug. "You're a firefighter, so of course you're here. We need some help, and you just sensed it."

Cadee laughed. "Or Jared told me."

"Ooh! Jared, huh? I wanna hear more."

Cadee fiddled with her shirt sleeves, looked over at Vince. Then she turned on a warm smile. "Mackenzie, this is my partner, Vince. What can we do to help?"

Mackenzie looked behind herself, then stepped onto the porch, closed the door. "Actually, Jared texted me a few minutes ago. He knew I needed help. He sent another trooper, and she is waiting in a van down the block. The Anchorage PD said they'd get these women somewhere safe until the wildfire's out. The bus driver was willing to drive them that far." She pointed away from Corner Store. "I somehow have to get three women and two kids to the van. *and* keep them from getting noticed and found by their abusive men."

Cadee nodded, bit her lower lip. "I have an idea. Are you all ready to go?"

Mackenzie nodded.

"Great. Go get them standing at the front door. Let me text Aunt Claire." She tapped into her phone, and Mackenzie jogged into the safe house.

A few seconds later, they heard Claire down by the bus at the Corner Store. "Bus leaving in three minutes. We're leaving in three minutes. Get on board. Now!" Cadee waved at Emma and Ava, who were already boarding.

Shouting, calling to one another, people gathered and boarded the bus.

Now was the time. Vince hustled to the back safe-house porch and grabbed some of the ladies' luggage. Behind him, Cadee took one baby in her arms and held a toddler's hand. Mackenzie led them to the van practically at a race walk. The women dove into the van while Vince loaded it up.

Mackenzie gave Cadee a hug and gave him a silly salute. She waved and climbed into the van, which took off.

Cadee turned around to the bus, where people were still loading their luggage. Emma stuck her head out the bus window and waved at them. Cadee waved back with both arms.

Vince just looked at Cadee. He'd seen her in training, in competition, facing fires. He hadn't seen her at home like this.

"Hey, we have to get out of here," he said.

"Wouldn't be dumb to do so."

"The friend of mine I ran across, you want to catch a ride with him?"

"Makes sense to me. We need to get back to base, get back with the team in case this wildfire explodes even more."

He started to call out for Nick but paused. He took a long look at Nick, standing by his sedan down the street, talking to someone.

"Yeah. Right." He frowned. What an intense conversation Nick was having. "Wait. That looks like Tristan Winters, Jamie's brother. I thought he was back in Copper Mountain." Already out of the Copper Mountain Clinic after his escape from the militia?

"Probably not him. His back is to us."

"True." He eyed his ex-partner, swaying back and forth in a heated conversation.

The other guy—in the usual jeans and T-shirt and boots of the men in the Alaska backcountry—turned their way. His beard had grown slightly beyond the scruff he'd had earlier, but this man must be Tristan. Had to be.

Vince was pretty sure Tristan saw them, recognized them. But then he turned, pulled on some earphones, and jogged away—practically sprinted away—and Nick jumped into the sedan and screamed off down the road.

"All right. Looks like we're hoofing it. We need to get out of here before the fire reaches us," Vince said.

SEVEN

WE'RE STILL PRETTY SMELLY, AREN'T we?" Cadee and Vince sat in the back of a rusty pickup truck, grateful to the driver who'd been kind enough to stop and pick them up.

"Yeah. If we'd ridden in Ingriq's bus or in Nick's sedan, we would've been in dishonor."

She waggled her eyebrows at him. "Or disrepute."

They fist-bumped. Instead of arguing. At least for now.

Cadee leaned back against the side panel of the truck bed, closed her eyes. Firefighting was a joy but an energy zap, until time to rest showed up. This mission had been crazy though. Salmon die-off, gunshots.

And they'd seen Vince's partner. Her ex. Yeah. Crazy.

But also, they'd found Emma and Ava. Saved Ingriq people.

She smiled, elbowed Vince. "This is why we're firefighters, isn't it?"

He nodded. "This is it. For sure." But his laugh lines were tight, his shoulders mostly up by his ears.

"What's wrong, Vince?"

"The DEA."

"Really? You mean Nick?"

Vince just sat there, his toes almost bouncing as he stared into space. "They have an arrest warrant for me."

She snorted. "You are so funny."

"No. It's real. Tucker messaged me from the office."

"What on earth do they want to arrest you for? Especially when you were in the DEA. And you're a firefighter now. What—"

"I don't know, something about drugs. It's the DEA," he snapped. Then he closed his eyes. "Sorry. It is nuts, but I don't know what it's about."

"Tucker's got you. Jade's got you. We all know it's insane."

"How do you know it's insane?"

"Because we know *you*." She put her hand on his shoulder. "We've all got you, Vince. Promise."

He tipped his chin, but he stared out into space.

The truck stopped at the intersection of the paved highway and the dirt road that led onto Midnight Sun jump base.

They hopped out of the bed of the truck and grabbed their fire packs. "Thanks, Henry!" Vince called, and the man gave a bit of a horn beep and drove off.

Vince put on a smile as they headed up the dirt road. "So, anyway," he said, "Ingriq was amazing. Do you wish you lived there instead of here?"

"Nope. I mean, I loved it there—still do—but..." She swirled around, flourishing her hands in the air. As if there was anywhere in the world she'd rather be than here, even if it made her turn into a character in *The Sound of Music*. "Look at that. There is beauty in Ingriq and in our base. How could I not love both places?"

"True. It's all beautiful, even in winter, you know?"

She smiled. "I do."

They walked quietly in the silence of the sun-bright evening for a few minutes.

"What's also cool about Midnight Sun firefighting," she said, "is that it's not just a place where you go to work, put in the hours, then go home."

He looked over at her, smiling. "That's why I'm glad I came here."

"I'm glad you came to Alaska too." She had to admit that.

Logan and Jamie sat outside at the firepit in the confluence of the men's, women's and married couples' dorms.

"You two survived each other, huh?" Logan called out.

"Of course we did, Logan." Vince laughed. "Hey, Jamie. How come you're *still* hanging around?" he teased back.

Cadee shoved his shoulder. "Seriously, how is everyone?"

Logan stood, coming over to shake Vince's hand, which turned into a bro hug. "The hotshots got the fire knocked down, and the bus driver is already picking up a few residents who don't have transportation. Hammer got Tristan to the hospital, but he's already out."

So Vince *had* seen Tristan in the village.

"Everyone else is safe except for Tori and Orion. Tucker is formulating a plan to go out and look for them."

"You're back!" JoJo came running out of the women's dorm and threw her arms around Cadee.

Skye followed at a more sedate pace, waving her hand in front of her nose. "You two stink!"

JoJo stepped back from Cadee. "You really do."

Jade came walking over from the married couples' cabin. "Until your text, I'd never heard of smokejumpers throwing themselves into a salmon die-off."

Cadee said, "I'm more concerned with why the fish were dead in the first place. It's the wrong time of year."

Jade nodded. "I'm glad you're back, you two. Gunshots and all. I expect a debrief later." She started walking toward the office building, turned back around. "Did the two of you work out everything?"

"Yes," said Vince.

"No," Cadee said at the same time.

Like they hadn't finally talked about Cap's death, about his DEA past?

Like they hadn't almost kissed?

Yeah, things weren't resolved between them.

Jade lasered them with her eyes. "Well, you're still partners. Get it together, you two." She gave them the you-better-behave mom stare until

Cadee wanted to squirm. Jade finally relaxed. "Go grab some grub before the mess hall closes."

Skye and JoJo followed Jamie and Logan across the runway to dinner.

Once they were alone again, Vince spun around to her. "How could you say no after all we did together, Cadee?"

She tipped up her chin. "How could you say yes? Apparently you think it's all hunky-dory when we still have a lot of things to work through."

"Like what?" His hands hung in the air in innocence.

Her stomach grumbled, but she badly wanted a shower—so much more than yet another argument with Vince. Besides, wide-leg sweats and her Midnight Sun sweatshirt sounded comfortable after this intense day.

"We'll talk after I shower."

Vince stood there, slack-jawed.

But she needed a shower. Cadee spun, grabbing her flight bag from the porch and heading to the women's cabin.

The shower at the Midnight Sun jump base only halfway spat out lukewarm water. But it felt good after the three-hour walk from Ingriq.

And the hour rushing around the village to help evacuees.

And the fight with Landon.

And seeing her ex.

And the dip in the slimy, stinky salmon die-off river.

She shuddered.

Yeah, what a crazy long day. No need for a fight with Vince.

But they'd helped the evacuees at Ingriq together.

They'd taken down Landon together.

She'd saved him from the river, and he'd saved her from it. The slime and stink had actually, somehow, made them laugh together.

Her phone buzzed as she stepped out of the shower. It was a text from Emma.

Emma

Surprise! Jade said Ava and I
could come here to spend time
with you. I'm having coffee in
the mess hall. Jade just told me
you arrived. Wanna join me?

Her sister was here? Cadee typed out a reply.

Cadee

I'll be there in five minutes.
Maybe get me a hamburger and
fries with the coffee?

Emma_____
You got it.

Cadee hurried into the charcoal sweats and the deep-blue Midnight Sun sweatshirt. She ran a brush through her hair and stood in front of the bathroom mirror, reached up to do her usual ponytail.

Stared at herself in the mirror and, for a second, saw Vince.

The look in his eyes back in the forest when he'd touched her face.

Nearly kissed her. Really?

Yes, definitely unfinished business.

She left the bathroom, sat on her cot, and slid on her tennis shoes as fast as she could. She needed to talk to Emma.

Her broken heart wasn't going to be able to stand much more of this, and Jade had flat out said she and Vince were still partners.

She wasn't going to get rid of him. Not without losing a big part of herself—again.

Cadee jogged across the runway and into the mess hall. Emma, her bright blonde hair in perfect braids, waved at her. She was sitting at the long pine table next to a cheeseburger and steamy coffee on the white tabletop covered with glass.

Hotshots and smokejumpers were scattered

around the room. Except Orion and Tori, which made their absence all the more noticeable. In one corner, Jade sat at a table with Tucker, their commander, talking intently. Figuring out a plan to find their friends?

Cadee gave her sister a side hug, slid onto the bench, and took a huge bite of cheeseburger.

"Vince and I almost kissed today."

Emma's face scrunched up. "What?"

"Just a second." She took another sip of coffee, set down the smokejumper coffee mug, ate another bite of the really great cheeseburger. "Okay, more than a second. Where's Ava?"

Emma flipped her hand in the air. "Coloring with Raine. The bus driver had to drive up here to take some hotshots back to Copper Mountain early tomorrow morning so they can head up to the fire. He offered me a ride. I called over and Jade said there were two extra cots in the women's cabin, so he brought us here, and we get to spend time with you. Now, quit changing the subject. You almost kissed? Spill, sis."

Cadee shook her head, her cheeks heating. "I saved Vince out of the gross river filled with dead salmon. Then I slipped in, and he got me out. It was really kind of funny. Maybe that's what we needed. We headed to Ingriq and, I don't know,

I finally felt like I should tell him what happened to his father."

"Wait." Emma's coffee splashed a little as she put it down. She put her hand on Cadee's arm. "You told me the whole story, but you never told him?"

Cadee dropped her head. "Logan gave him the basics, told him to ask me."

"He didn't?"

"Not until today." And she was pretty sure that's why he'd been picking fights with her since he joined Midnight Sun.

"But you didn't tell him before now?"

She shook her head. "It never seemed like the right time, and the words always got stuck in my throat." She shoved the cheeseburger into her mouth, took a huge bite. Couldn't Emma just listen?

Stop it, Cadee. Emma *was* listening.

She took a drink of coffee. They both had their hands around their coffee mugs like they used to when Mom would make them hot chocolate on a bad day. *God, help me here.*

"I'm sorry, Emma," she said. "Your house might have burned down today, and now you're staying here with Ava. It can't be easy facing living in temporary housing with a daughter." Cadee could at least act like she wanted her sister here. "I'm glad I found you today."

"Me too." Emma smiled. "Now keep talking."

Another drink of coffee. "The day Cap died, I just couldn't tell Vince what'd happened. Not even at the funeral."

Emma put her hand back on Cadee's arm. "You were scared Vince would hate you."

"But mostly, my voice simply wouldn't work. I was just . . ."

"Grieving."

Cadee swallowed. "But he was so angry when I . . . couldn't . . . talk to him that he broke up with me. Now that we're both here on the Midnight Sun crew, we can't seem to get along. I'm sure everyone is sick of the constant bickering and arguing, which is why Jade forced us to be partners at this wildfire."

"And how has that gone?"

"Actually, we work really well together. When I told Vince the whole story, we talked. It was like old times. And we almost kissed." Cadee took another huge bite of her burger so she didn't have to say more.

Would he really have kissed her back? Their relationship was strained, but maybe their feelings that started back in Ember hadn't changed as much as she'd thought.

Emma chuckled. "You can't tell where things are going just from that." She squeezed Cadee's arm and took her cup of coffee into both hands. "You need to talk to him. Figure out between you where it's going so you don't get your heart broken all over again."

Cadee took a drink of coffee too. "Vince told me something else." She wrapped both hands back around her coffee mug, hardly able to say the words aloud. And yet she could jump out of a plane into a fire, no problem.

Emma duck-faced her lips, waiting. "So, tell me already."

"He told me the DEA has a warrant out for his arrest."

Emma's coffee cup clumped down on the table. "What for?"

"Not for sure, but it is the DEA. Something about drugs, most likely."

Emma's shoulders dropped. "I'm sorry, Cadee."

The knots holding Cadee's heart hostage tightened. But she wouldn't let them. Cadee blew out a breath. "No. It's crazy. He's a good guy, even if we don't get along. And he's been out of the DEA for, well, a few years." She shrugged. "At least since Ember. Why would they come after him now?"

"Remember that idiot, Phil, back in high school?"

She glared at Emma. "Yeah. Vince is not Phil. I trust Vince." Her shoulders dropped. "But, yeah, the DEA thing has snuck in that one percent of doubt."

Emma pointed at her. "Let me get this straight. Vince trusts you, opens up. I know things were, I don't know, craggy between you. Trust has to be rebuilt, of course." Emma sighed. "You're so busy trying to keep from being hurt again—even a little one percent."

Cadee stared at her sister. Then she slumped over her plate and reached for her cheeseburger, but she let it go when Jamie came over and plopped down at the table.

"Am I interrupting something?" Jamie glanced between them.

Emma opened her mouth to answer, so Cadee cut her off. "No, nothing important."

"Can I pick your brains since you're locals?" Jamie took a long sip of her coffee. When they both nodded, she continued. "While I was here, I thought I'd look into how to donate to the Midnight Sun crew, and it looks like you guys pull from the Northern Lights Higher Education Foundation for your recruits. So I nosed around, and when I dug below the surface, the organization seemed a bit sketchy."

Emma frowned. "Do you donate to it, Cadee?"

"I do." This was the first she'd heard about it not being legit.

"I mean, on the surface, eighty percent of the donations goes to scholarships, and twenty percent builds your retirement," Jamie said. "But I don't see any scholarships being given, nor can I tell where the twenty percent has gone."

Cadee frowned. "I have statements showing what I put into it. Are you saying we should quit donating to the program?"

"No. Hang loose. I tend to be a skeptic on charities, so I probably shouldn't have said anything. Helping Alaskan students is a positive thing." Jamie thought for a moment. "I'm going to reach out to Skye though. She told me about it."

Cadee stared into her mug as she swished her coffee around. "Vince donates to it as well. We all do. If he trusts it, then I'm not worried at all."

Her sister tapped her fingers on the table.

Cadee glanced over and saw Emma's grin. She shook her head. "Yes, I trust him."

She wondered if they would've kissed on the

trail if militia guy hadn't interrupted them with a gunshot.

But the biggest question was why she missed the long conversations with Vince and the warmth of his shoulder next to hers.

Emma took her hand across the table. "Let's go enjoy the firepit. You'll be up and out fighting fires again first thing in the morning, so we might not get much chance to hang out for a while. I'll text Raine to join us or at least to bring out Ava. That kid might have asthma, but she loves firepits."

"Sure." And Cadee absolutely would not look for Vince.

Not at all.

Yeah, they'd said they would talk later. And this was later.

But she was suddenly afraid of the answer to the question—where did they go from here?

"Hey, Tucker," Vince said as he walked into the commander's office in the admin building. "Logan kind of followed me in, if that's okay."

Tucker smiled. "If it's okay with you, it's okay with me."

He bobbed his head. Yeah. Tucker almost

certainly wanted to talk about the warrant. But Logan was a friend.

Logan shook Tucker's hand, and they all sat down. "Do we know anything about Orion and Tori yet?"

"Nothing yet," Tucker answered. "Jade saw them land together, so I'm certain they're on their way to the base. We just haven't been able to get ahold of them. Maybe their radio got damaged."

Logan nodded. "Maybe we could reach out to the National Forest Service."

"And to our contacts at the Alaska Division of Forestry & Fire Protection," Vince added.

Tucker typed into his phone. "Yes. That's perfect. I'll call and ask them to keep eyes out for them."

Tucker tapped his fingers on his desk, put his phone in his pocket, looked over at Logan, then back at Vince. "We need to talk about the warrant the DEA has out for you."

"I figured that's why you called me in. I know you need to report my whereabouts. Not going to blame you at all."

"No. I know you, Vince. I'm not calling anyone. I haven't officially been made aware of the warrant. DEA can show up and cuff you if they want you in custody."

Another person who believed in him. Vince didn't even ask how Tucker had found out. Best not to know. Then Tucker wouldn't end up in the DEA doghouse.

Logan tipped his head Vince's direction. "You didn't tell me why you left the DEA."

Tucker just nodded, waiting for his answer.

"Okay. My time in the agency isn't a secret. I just don't like talking about it. The thing is that they wanted to charge me with money laundering. But their evidence was wrong, and I was totally cleared. I quit because, despite the correct facts, I still got those cynical looks from the other agents. They didn't stop. I finally quit the DEA to clear my name for good. It was, um, difficult. My mentor and partner, Nick Atwood, didn't doubt my innocence for one moment. He reminded me of Dad being up here, fighting fires, saving lives and property. So I knew my new calling. I hit the Ember training program—"

"Met Cadee," Logan teased.

Yeah. Cadee.

Vince nodded. "Then I ended up here."

Tucker blew out a breath. "Wish you'd been up here earlier. Your dad would have loved working with you."

His Adam's apple bobbed, and he couldn't speak past the lump in his throat.

Logan thumped his shoulder.

"Okay, Vince," Tucker said. "You're going to go out with the team tomorrow if that fire spurs off toward Rough Campground. I'll talk to Rio at the FBI and clear this up. Don't worry about it. Sooner or later, they'll realize you have no part in whatever this is."

"I'd really like to get a forty-eight-hour leave and solve it, Tucker."

Tucker leaned back in his chair. "I'll think about it."

"Thanks."

Maybe.

Because Cadee had been terrorized enough. He wouldn't drag her into more trouble.

This wasn't like simply waiting for a storm to end. He needed to fix it himself.

He stood and shook hands with Tucker. Logan did as well.

"Pray for Tori and Orion, please."

"Of course," Logan said.

Vince didn't say anything.

He and Logan silently walked down the stairs.

Vince hit the push bar at the bottom, and they went out into the Alaskan air, which had a light, crisp, wintergreen smell of birch, and headed across the parking lot to the men's cabin.

"I keep praying for Tori and Orion," Logan said. "'God is our refuge and strength, a very present help in trouble.'"

Vince looked at Logan. They'd fought fires together in Montana. Become real friends, talked like real friends. But he couldn't talk to him about faith. Or his lack of it.

He grunted.

Logan frowned. "What's going on?"

Vince just shrugged. "Don't want to talk about it. I want to get out of here, solve the DEA thing. Tucker didn't give me the days off to do so, wants me to just wait on him to decide sometime."

"'The Lord will fight for you, and you shall hold your peace.' Exodus. Tucker's a good guy."

"Yeah. Prayer. Who's solving the DEA issue? Who's out looking for Tori and Orion?"

Logan crossed his arms. "Praying for Tori and Orion isn't a doable thing for you?"

Vince scratched at his shoulder.

Logan gently put his hand on Vince's arm, stopped him.

He tried to ignore the topic Logan wanted to delve into, but his friend was waiting for an answer. And Vince couldn't honestly just say something positive. "God. Doesn't. Answer."

"You hate God?"

"Neutral. Nothing more or less."

"Ah. I get it, my friend. If you want to be neutral toward God because your dad died, you can be. God's eyes are on you though. Because He loves you. Like Cap taught you, demonstrated to you."

"Logan, we're friends. I trust you. I don't need this."

Logan dipped his head, then his gentle gaze met Vince's. His voice was soft. "We all take time to grieve. God understands your grief. He's waiting on you."

Vince's mouth opened.

Logan patted Vince's shoulder, then strode out of the cabin.

God was waiting on him to work through his grief.

His breath suddenly whooshed out of him.

Logan was a hundred percent accurate. *We all take time to grieve.* He certainly did. And would continue to. It was *his* dad who'd died, *his* grief that he'd been concerned with. Everything *he* had lost.

But had he given Cadee time to grieve? *He was like a father to me.*

His stomach twisted.

He accepted that she'd finally shared the story with him this morning.

But he owed her an apology.

Vince headed toward the mess hall—he didn't want to wait until the morning.

Soon as he stepped off the porch, he spotted her.

There she was with Emma and Ava at the fire-pit. It was encircled by a stack of stones, the fire bright and inviting, even in the semi-light of the civil twilight of the evening.

He paused, looking at the fire warming Cadee's face, the three of them giggling, Ava dancing around. He wanted a future with Cadee so badly he felt it deep in his heart. But he wasn't going to ask her to give up this and face the mess of his life.

Cadee looked over and waved. "Hey, Vince."

"Uncle Vince!" Ava yelled, throwing herself into his arms as he walked up to the fire.

He spun her around till she giggled, then lowered her to the ground, his cheeks flushed with embarrassment. "Hey, kiddo. Hey, Emma. Didn't know you two were coming to base camp."

Emma looked back and forth between him and

Cadee. "Um, hi, Vince. Yeah, we've had a great talk. Love the bonfire." She clapped her hands together with a smile. "Come on, Ava, it's time for a bedtime story."

"Yay." Ava's reddish-blonde ponytail swung back and forth as she made ballerina spins all the way to her mom and took her hand.

Yeah, they'd been talking about him.

This was embarrassing.

Emma ran off, hand in hand with her daughter, and Vince sat on the log next to Cadee.

"Ahem. Sorry about that." She smiled.

"So Emma knows—"

"That we almost kissed? She does."

His eyes darted around to see if anyone was near enough to hear. "Yeah. So I owe you an apology."

"An apology because you didn't mean to almost kiss me?"

"Yeah. No." Was his head spinning? He wished that kiss had happened. Things had felt so right back in Ember. He wanted that back. But he didn't need to drag her into his problems. She'd had enough terror.

He needed to figure out some way to clear his name.

He had a DEA arrest over his head.

He had jail over his head.

"I'm sorry I blamed you for Dad's death. Of course you tried to save him. You're Cadee Moore."

She gulped hard, her hand on her chest.

He looked down at his feet, then up into her eyes. "You lost him too. I'm sorry for your loss, Cadee."

Her breath hitched. "No one ever . . ." She scooched a little closer to him, looked deep into his eyes. "Thank you, Vince."

An eagle flew overhead, piping high notes. The fire in the firepit was crackling gently, filling the air with the scent of the birch. The birch leaves rustled in the breeze.

Cadee smiled, her eyes closed. Then she grinned, opened her eyes. "We should talk about that almost kiss."

But he couldn't. "Cadee . . . we're not ready for this."

"Actually, I get it. You may not be ready—*we* may not be ready—for a kiss. But we are definitely out of the enemy zone." She smiled up at him. "Solidly into friendship."

He looked into the fire. "Look, I'm glad we did move out of that twenty-four-seven quarreling—"

Cadee snorted.

"—bickering, arguing, driving Jade and the crew crazy."

Were they holding hands? He pulled his hand out of hers.

Her grin faded.

"Cadee. We did move beyond all that. Finally. But I need to straighten out the junk with the DEA."

She leaned forward, close, her elbows resting on her knees. "Yeah. And I have your back."

"You can't."

"I can. I will."

"Cadee. It's..." He rubbed his eyes. "*Somebody* is after me. I don't want them after you. I need to figure it all out, put a stop to it, if we're going to be free to have a future together."

"I have your back, Vince."

He continued. "I could end up in prison. For a federal crime. You don't need that."

He stood, walked back to the men's cabin. He hated it. But he had to.

First thing tomorrow, he needed to talk to Nick.

EIGHT

CADEE WAS THE FIRST ONE OUT THE door at the end of the early morning briefing—a new spur of the fire was heading out toward Rough Campground.

No way was she going to stick around and have to face Vince again. Not after their conversation last night. She'd been such an idiot thinking he might want to get back together.

She would've helped him. Stood by him.

But he'd thrown it all in her face. Forget Vince. Just fight fires.

Logan jogged up beside her. "Everything okay?"

She glanced over at him and saw Vince going the opposite way, down the hall. Avoiding her?

She tore her eyes away from the guy determined to run away from her.

Cadee said, "Yeah, just anxious to get out there and fight fire. I'm gonna make sure my gear is checked over, ready to go."

He volleyed his phone from hand to hand. "I meant is everything okay with Vince."

She felt the blood rush into her cheeks. "No offense, but I don't think Vince and I are any of your business. He's got enough to worry about."

He shifted feet. "I only meant to say that Vince is struggling with his faith."

"What faith? He doesn't even believe in God." She was struggling as well, if she was honest, even if she hadn't turned her back on God.

Logan said, "That's where I think you're wrong. He knows God is real, he just needs to trust in Him."

Cadee couldn't help remembering her sister's words from the night before. *Trust has to be rebuilt.* "We all have a lot to work out. It's part of life."

His gaze pierced her. "'Let all bitterness and wrath and anger and clamor and slander be put away from you, along with all malice.'"

Were they even talking about Vince anymore?

Her throat squeezed. "Ephesians Four. Thanks for basically telling me I'm a horrible person."

"Cadee—"

She turned and pushed through the door.

"That's not what I meant. I said 'let.' That verse is all about grace. *Grace*." Logan's voice drifted down the stairs toward her, but she descended faster with each step until she was running. Those were *not* tears running down her face.

Cadee took the long way around the office, giving herself a minute to pull it together. At the side of the building, she stopped, panting, elbows on knees. She wiped her face and straightened up. Leaned against the wall, trying to hum her favorite hymn, "Amazing Grace," but the notes didn't seem to want to come. All she could remember was a line about fear, and not how she could get rid of it.

Was she really afraid of getting hurt again?

In keeping the crew at a distance, had she turned into an awful person?

She kicked off the side of the office building and walked to the cabins so she could grab a couple of protein bars for later. Raine and Sanchez, a couple of the hotshots, passed her, mid conversation.

". . . I heard him say it. An arrest warrant. Can you believe that?" Raine shook her head.

Sanchez said, "What is he going to do, Cadee?"

"He was asking Tucker for a couple of days to go figure out what was going on. Like he's gonna find evidence or something? I don't know. Tucker didn't give him an answer yet. Logan told him that verse from Exodus. *The Lord will fight for you, and you shall hold your peace.* I don't think Vince liked the idea of doing nothing, waiting for God to fix it."

Sanchez didn't say anything in response to that. The two women climbed the steps to the women's cabin.

Cadee stared at the men's cabin, thinking about that text from Vince about Logan's Exodus advice and Tucker deciding not to give him the days off.

Was he going to leave?

Without thinking about it, Cadee jogged to the men's cabin. The guys were practically moving in choreography as they prepared to head out on the bus to the fire they'd been briefed on.

Good thing she had already checked her gear. Because she needed to talk to Vince.

But she didn't see him.

On the far side of the cabin, by the RV spots,

Vince tossed a duffel bag into the backseat of his vehicle.

She hurried over. "Hey."

"Just a sec." He backed out of his truck with a soft smile. "Hey, Cadee."

"Whatcha doing, Vince?"

"I had to get my charger plugged into my truck. Wanted my playlist for the road."

Her stomach dropped. "You're really leaving?"

He leaned his back up against the truck. "I need to find out what on earth is going on with that DEA warrant. I can't wait for Tucker to give me some days off. I can't just pretend it doesn't exist."

"We have a fire." She looked at her watch. "Wheels up in twenty minutes."

She wanted to tell him that people could die and he was being selfish. But wouldn't she do the same in his position? Fighting fires and not knowing if he'd be a free man tomorrow would be hard.

Then again, even though he'd rejected her and their relationship, maybe she just wanted him nearby. Didn't want to let him go again.

He pinched his lips together and started back to the cabin. She followed him to his room and stood by the door. He said, "My mind just started wandering during the briefing, and I realized I can't fight the fire with everyone. It's time for me to figure out what's going on before the DEA comes and yanks me out of a wildfire fight. I followed my dad here, and now I'm *not* going to lose this job because someone doesn't know what they're talking about."

"I need to tell you something."

He sighed. "I need to get on the road."

"I promise this has a point." Did he think she was trying to get him back? He'd made it clear where they stood, but she still cared about him. Cadee wandered over and sank onto the edge of the bed.

He shifted his suitcase, sat next to her on the cot.

"I was made fun of a lot. One girl in elementary told the teacher I stole her lunch—"

He laughed. Hard. "You stole someone's lunch?"

Her fake glare didn't last more than a second before a laugh escaped from her. "Of course not. It was an all-out lie—a good lie—so the teacher believed that girl. I was banned from the amusement park field trip and spent the field trip day writing an essay. Same girl in high school tattled to my prom date that I got my dress at a thrift store. He ghosted me."

"Ouch."

She nodded. "I spent the evening at the indoor climbing gym. The owner comped me my ticket and offered me a job. I spent all my off-hours training to become a hotshot after that."

Vince played with the handle of his suitcase, listening but obviously eager to go.

She scanned the knots and small splits in the logs of the cabin for a long moment. She swallowed. "After I came back up to Alaska to be a smokejumper, I was sitting at the mess hall table here once, trying to figure out my bank account. Your dad sat down and helped me. He taught me how to handle money, week by week. He taught me how to, uh, unlearn bad habits I learned from my parents."

Vince reached forward, covered her hand with his. "Dad was a smart man."

She threw back her head, laughing. "But he was *not* an accountant."

Vince's mouth curled up to one side. "He was a firefighter."

She pulled her hand out from under his. "And that's it, Vince. He was a real man who knew real things, like budgets. And he lived real things—he lived the truth of what he believed. He died trusting God would take care of him, no matter what."

"Adulting and faith. That was Dad." He stood up, grabbed his suitcase. "I've gotta go. Tell everyone thanks for understanding. And thank you for understanding too. See you soon."

Vince was going to walk away. But she had to finish her point and say what he needed to hear, or he might not come back.

He dipped his head and strode toward the front door.

"Vince!" Cadee called from behind him.

The ring of that voice stopped him dead in his tracks. He wanted to stay. Didn't she know how tempting she made it to give up what he knew he needed to do and stick around?

For her. The way she'd snorted a laugh at the firepit last night.

The way she'd leaned into his space, promised to have his back.

The way she'd held his hand.

He wanted to stay, pull her into his arms. But he wasn't free to do that.

Not yet.

"Your dad laid a strong foundation of faith for me. There's no way he didn't tell you what he believed."

He set down his suitcase. So that was the point she was taking the long way toward. He turned around. "So what? He's gone." But he knew she saw a sheen of grief in his eyes.

"The Bible I use? He gave it to me."

"Wide margins for making notes?"

Cadee chuckled. "Yep."

Logan jogged past them. "Fifteen minutes to wheels up," he called on his way out the door.

Maybe the DEA would believe the lies against him like the teacher had believed the lie that Cadee had stolen someone's lunch. If this was their last conversation . . .

Vince turned around. "Is your fire pack ready?"

She nodded. "I put it on the bus before the briefing."

He rocked on his heels. "Okay. I'm listening. But I need to go. You need to go."

"You followed your dad here. You're leaving the fight against fires?"

"I want to clear my name, not get dragged down into the mud and wind up in prison because I didn't fight for my innocence."

With a sigh, she deliberately siphoned off her frustration. Her deep-blue eyes gentled. "Clear your name?"

His heart beat hard. Yeah, she'd caught that.

Would she walk away if he told her? Probably. But this was Cadee he was talking to. Even if this wasn't a coffee date like they used to have.

He sat back down on his cot, next to her.

"Tell me, Vince. I'm here," she said.

Okay. He would then. "My mom was an embezzler. Of course, she ended up in prison. That's, I think, why I wanted to join law enforcement, because I didn't like the idea of other kids going through what I had. Having to live with keeping secrets for her and then watching her whole fabricated life fall down around her. It ruined my dad. That's why he was so careful with money. After college, I applied for, and was offered, a DEA slot, and I wanted it. Bad. But Dad wanted me to join him as a firefighter so I could continue his legacy. We fought. A lot."

He shook his head. "It wasn't that I didn't want to do this. I just wanted to be a Fed *more*." He lifted his hands in admission. "Anyway, I just wanted to show that our family was not criminal, but that we stood for what is right."

"Fighting your dad, because you want to fight for what is right?"

"Hadn't exactly thought of it that way."

She shrugged. "Not sure Cap was against you fighting for justice."

"But then Logan gave me that sage advice, supposedly, about saying nothing. Letting God fight for me." He shook his head. That had never been his reality. He'd had to fight for *everything*.

"And he can't be right?"

Vince said, "My dad was just sure I had a calling from God to be a hotshot and then a smokejumper, not law enforcement. But I wasn't into God at that point."

Or now. The ping of truth raced up his spine.

He hadn't thought of it *that way*, either.

Vince continued. "I joined the DEA in California after college, had a great partner—Nick, the guy I talked to in Ingriq. We had solid success against the criminal world. We were clicking, getting results. Then I got accused of money laundering."

Cadee's jaw dropped, then she snapped it shut. "Really?"

He scrubbed his hand through his hair. "Yeah. I suspect these new charges are related to that old case."

Cadee's eyes widened.

"So late last night I asked Jamie to do some digging for me."

"Jamie rocks."

He nodded. "Looking into the old case, she

discovered that someone—she hasn't tracked down who yet—had loaded a bank account with money laundered through real estate. The DEA thought it was mine since I'd owned an account in the same bank. They added that 'coincidence' to my mom's embezzlement and dug into my past. Found nothing. Dropped it. But now it's reopened because these new charges against me include money laundering. Again. They're trying to make two and three make four."

"I know you didn't—you don't—do criminal things, much less money laundering." She set her hand on his arm. "Please tell me you believe that."

He couldn't stop the small laugh that puffed out. "Of course I do. But that's exactly why I need to clear my reputation with the DEA."

"Speaking of . . ." A throat being cleared interrupted him, and they looked up.

Skye was walking by, clipboard in hand. "Everyone filled me in on what's happening. I guess they didn't want a conflict of interest, but the truth is, I don't like it when good people are treated like criminals when they've done nothing wrong. My husband is an FBI agent. Can I fill him in? He might be able to help."

Skye didn't seem to have a doubt that Rio would clear this up. No one except Vince's partner had ever looked at him like he was an honest man after the whole money-laundering thing— the reason he'd left the DEA.

More false accusations. But they'd had no evidence, so he'd never been arrested. What had changed now?

He turned to stare at the mountains and a plume of smoke snaking into the sky and creating a haze on the horizon that smelled like a bonfire. Rather than being a smokejumper like his dad had always wanted, clearing his name, it turned out, was *still* his job. Whether he liked it or not.

He smiled at Skye. "Appreciate it. I'll let you know."

She stood silently appraising him. "You sure?"

"Thanks, Skye."

"Promise me you'll let me know if you do need Rio?"

"I will."

She turned, looking over her shoulder as she walked away. "Jade moved up the leave time. Five minutes and we're outta here."

He grabbed his suitcase handle, stood. "You ready to go?"

No answer. He turned back around. Cadee's eyes were squeezed shut, her arms crossed tight over her stomach.

He sat back down. "Cadee, I will be back."

She took a long, deep breath, then looked up into his eyes with a sad smile. "Okay. But will you be back to your faith as well, or just firefighting?"

"Wow. That's harsh."

She only nodded. "You made it clear last night where we stand, but I still care about you."

"Okay, look, Dad taught me to parachute years ago as a surprise birthday present. Fun day. He seemed different. Of course he wanted me to fight fires, but I wanted to be in the DEA. That was the first time he really listened to me about it. And I listened to him when he told me how Christ accepted him, flaws and all, and so he'd accepted Christ. And he told me that Christ had that same love for me." He laughed at the way that sounded. "It felt like 'Jesus Loves Me' simplicity."

Cadee lightly elbowed him. "Which Jesus is."

Jade shouted into the cabin, "Hammer, where are you? Come help JoJo load the Pulaskis and McLeods onto the bus. Skye too. Don't know what we're walking into."

"Coming!" Hammer ran past them out the front door.

Vince turned to Cadee. "The 'Jesus Loves Me' forgiveness and the love of God that Dad opened up to me are simple. I get it. But living it is not simple. I just can't . . ."

Her voice cracked. "Grief."

"Yeah." He shifted. "Cadee, I don't know if I will return to my faith."

She flicked a finger across her cheek. Swiping away an imaginary tear? She didn't need to cry for him.

"I haven't turned my back on what my father taught me." His throat constricted. He wouldn't lie to anyone, especially Cadee.

"When he died," she said, "I had an even greater impetus to rush in, save people, do everything. Yeah, my faith isn't gone, and I'm trying to trust Him. But it's still hard not to struggle with bitterness. Cap is gone. You broke up with me. So I am just, I don't know, focused on the job, trying even harder to do *everything*."

His head lowered. "I am sorry."

She put her hand over his. "Forgiven. Christ's grace is bigger than fear, and I don't want to wallow in bitterness."

He'd always loved that calloused firefighting hand resting on his. Vince rolled his shoulders, then looked in her eyes, deep, his breath speeding up. He couldn't not say it. "I want to see where that kiss we could've had will lead, but too much is up in the air."

She turned pink, tipped up her chin. "I do too. No matter what happens."

His stomach clenched, just like before their first kiss, when they'd started dating at Ember during training.

Cadee stepped back, her hand on his heart for a moment.

Cold shivered down his spine . . . like she was gone.

Her voice was shaky. "Why don't we pray together about what's going on? Whenever I need to let God take away the edge of my bitterness, I pray. It doesn't have to be now. Whenever you're ready."

He could do nothing but nod. "Later."

Suddenly, Jade shouted in the open front door. "Wheels up in two minutes. Head out. Now."

Cadee dipped her head in a nod and ran for the front door.

He reached for his suitcase and his fire pack, walked out behind her toward his truck.

He was an idiot.

He jogged back up the steps of the porch, dumped his suitcase inside the door and chased after her toward the bus.

When he caught up to her, she looked over in surprise.

"I'll follow up with my DEA partner later." He'd sound crazy trying to explain it, but Vince just couldn't walk away from her right now. "I followed Dad here. I'm staying. For now."

Was Tucker right that the Feds would figure out the truth and he'd be in the clear?

It seemed crazy, but could he really let God fight for him?

A BOUT A HALF MILE AWAY FROM THE
fire, the bus pulled off to the side of the road, and
Cadee piled out with Jade, Logan, Skye, JoJo, and
Hammer. The rest pulled up in the bus behind them.

They weren't near Rough Campground exactly,
but they were going to keep the fire away from it.
Camp kids and church groups and high-school
sports teams all loved the place. Ava had had her
first week of camp there earlier this summer. She'd
learned how to shoot a bow and arrow and even
got to go mushroom hunting.

From the underbody of the bus, Vince and
Cadee grabbed their Pulaskis. Hammer took his
McLeod, hooked it to his belt, and pulled out a
shovel. Jade grabbed an axe—she loved to swing

the thing. Single file, they headed from the highway and into the trees.

Toward the fire.

The smoke changed to a thick, dark gray, and Jade upped the speed to double time.

Who knew what they were walking into?

Logan in front of her and Hammer behind her, Vince bringing up the tail. Yeah, they were ready. Vince with them . . . she smiled. It felt right to work side by side. The things between them could just, what? Percolate? Yep. That was it. Percolate.

About ten minutes later, they reached the edge of the fire. The fire wasn't big, but it was popping, flinging embers into the air. The embers were fading as they fell on the wildflowers and moss, but it would only take a small increase in the fire's strength to explode its size.

Not today.

Cadee held her Pulaski at the ready.

Jade stood behind them and pulled a Kestrel out of her pocket, holding it up to judge the humidity, wind speed, and other fire weather. "Nothing new. We've got to focus on getting to the cabin or house or whatever building the report says is the source of this thick gray smoke." She pointed to where they needed to scrape their fire line. "Let's dig in. Three feet deep, a quarter mile wide. Logan, stand back and keep your eyes open for any flames that think they want to pop over."

The rest of them spread out and scraped away the debris on the forest floor to starve the fire.

Vince cranked his chain saw and went to work against the trunk of a fallen tree that lay across the mapped-out fire line. Logan carted the pieces off into the woods across from the fire while the sound of the rasping and slashing of Pulaskis and McLeods from the rest of the team was like a percussion ensemble underneath his chain saw. Cadee loved being a part of it.

The fire wasn't happy about its fuel being taken away. It sizzled and puffed, but it got smaller and smaller.

A breeze stirred up and blew a small eddy of embers to flame up across the fire line at the periphery of Cadee's vision.

"Got this," Logan called, and the digging of his shovel and throwing of dirt over the flame joined the thrum of the ensemble. "It's out, but come take a look, Jade. There's the cabin on fire, right over here."

Cadee kept her Pulaski moving but took a look in the direction Logan pointed. There it was—a rustic log cabin nearly hidden from sight by the debris and naturally fallen trees that were on fire around it. But it was clearly the source. The rest of the fire was almost down to a sizzle already, now that they had scraped away its fuel and buried the embers. But the cabin was still burning.

Someone leave a fire burning in the fireplace?

Jade slung her Pulaski over her shoulder, and she and Logan jogged up the hill to take a look down at the cabin. "I think there's someone in there," she called, shading her eyes against the sun.

The window glass began to pop as the fire took down the building. There was definitely a shadow in there. Had to be a person.

"Vince, bring your chain saw. Cadee, shovel," Jade called.

They sprinted over, leaving Hammer and Logan at work at the fire line.

Vince's chain saw quickly released a burning piece of the wooden door, and Cadee focused on the job at hand, using her shovel to pull the pieces a little away from the cabin and piling dirt on them to put it out.

Behind them, there was a crash. Logan screamed, and then a thump.

Cadee snuck a glance behind her to see Logan rolling like a man on fire. The thump had come from a burning tree limb that had broken off and fallen on him. Hammer's Pulaski dropped to the ground, and he and Jade ran over to Logan.

But Logan stood, holding a Pulaski. "I didn't catch on fire. Not hurt. I'm ready to go. Let's keep that fire out of the woods." But he paled, swayed just a little.

Jade stepped up to him. "Logan. Sit. Down."

"I'm here to help, Chief."

"Logan, that limb struck you on the *head*. You could be injured in a way we can't see. Just sit here. For a minute. Maybe two. Cadee and Vince have the cabin, Hammer and I have the fire line. Now sit down."

Cadee was glad to see Hammer help him sit against a spruce tree.

Hammer and Jade moved to the cabin with their fire line work to make sure the fire couldn't leave the building.

Sweat dribbled down her back, even in the sixty-degree Alaskan weather, as Vince cut off burning piece after burning piece of the door. Until the hole was big enough. The chain saw noise faded, and she dumped one last shovelful of dirt on the last piece of door.

"Going in, Jade," he said.

"With him," Cadee added.

"Careful, you two. It's still on fire."

Cadee pulled her fire hat over her head, followed Vince in. They sank to the floor beside a man, who was tied up in rope.

Cadee patted his pants that were beginning to catch on fire—there were going to be some burns. Turned him over.

"It's Tristan," she gasped. "Jamie's brother." She put her hand on his back. "He's breathing." Barely, but he'd been lying in the smoke of the fire that was still taking down the cabin. If they hadn't made it in, he'd have had no hope of surviving.

"This tiny building is going to be gone in a short time. We gotta get him out of here," Vince said. "And ourselves."

He draped the man over his shoulder in a fireman's carry and beelined out, Cadee following. Once they were away from the cabin, Vince gently laid the man down on a thick bed of moss under the birch trees that hadn't caught fire. He untied him. "What is he even doing here?"

Jade knelt beside him and rubbed his chest to try to stir him into consciousness. It worked. Tristan sucked in several breaths.

"Easy, Tristan," Cadee urged, then helped him pull himself to sitting, his back against a tree trunk.

Behind him, Vince caught her eye and silently

tipped his chin at the black-and-red headband Tristan was wearing.

Which looked like the headband he'd taken a picture of by the salmon die-off river where they'd met Landon.

The cabin collapsed in the whoosh of an implosion. Ash swirled around. The team moved in, chopping the wood into pieces and dumping dirt on the rubble so the embers would die.

"Logan, get Tristan some water and call in a helo for him," Jade ordered while they worked.

"Got it, Chief." He pulled out his phone, grabbed a water out of his fire pack.

Covered in ash, Tristan took it, but he was clearly weak and didn't have enough lung power for speaking yet. His hands shook, the water dribbling down his chin.

"Are you okay, man? What were you doing in that house?" Logan crouched in front of him as Cadee walked back over to them.

Vince paused his chain saw, taking a drink of water from his water bottle. He jerked his head toward the injured man. "Hey, Cadee," he said softly. "We did see Tristan in Ingriq, didn't we? Talking to my DEA partner, right?"

Cadee grabbed a deep drink of water. "We

did. Unless he's got a random twin brother or something."

"Yeah, right." He jerked his chain saw to life. "Tell Jade."

Meanwhile, Logan had moved away, his voice rising. "Midnight Sun smokejump team one," he said, his lips twisted. "Need a helo. Two injuries. One severe, civilian." He paced under the birch, one that had not turned black because of the cabin's fire, talking about where the helo could land.

Cadee moved to work the portion of the cabin where Jade was working. "Tristan . . . pretty sure Vince and I saw him during the Ingriq evacuation."

Jade's eyebrows rose, and she nodded. "I'll pass that along."

Logan walked up. "We're set to meet the helicopter about a half mile away." He pointed in the general direction north.

"Okay." Jade called out, "Hammer, you and I will take turns pulling this gentleman to the helo, and Logan is going to come with us. Let's get him packed up on the Sked. Cadee and Vince, stay here and make sure there are no more popups. We'll all head back to the west where the bus dropped us."

"Yes, Chief," she said.

Vince handed over the Sked, and they unrolled it next to Tristan. "You okay, man?" he asked, and Tristan nodded, his breath still rough.

Hammer stood at Tristan's head, reached down under his shoulders, and pulled him onto the Sked. Then he and Jade clicked the buckles around him and adjusted the straps.

Hammer pulled the Sked behind him as they headed to the clearing to meet the helicopter.

Cadee and Vince walked around the former cabin with shovels, occasionally tossing another shovelful of dirt where it seemed to want to heat up but didn't.

"Finally looks like this fire is broken down."

Vince wiped the sweat from his forehead, grabbed another bottle of water. "Actually, it still seems hot on the inside of the leftover cabin." He stepped into the leftovers, stirring them around with his shovel so they couldn't randomly heat up without their notice. He squatted down.

Cadee squatted next to him. "What do you see?"

"That Tristan guy doesn't smoke, right?"

"I don't know. Why?"

He reached down and pulled a cigarette butt out of the ashes, held it up to show her.

"Huh."

They both used their gloved fingers to search through the area for the next ten or fifteen minutes. They found melted earphones where Tristan had been lying. And a piece of melted rubber—had to be the vestiges of a rubber band.

"Three or four boxes of matches rubber-banded, cigarette stuck in the middle. Presto. Fire starter."

"Yeah. Arson. Maybe the militia?" she suggested. "That means they're trying to kill him as well, and they tried to cover it up by making us believe the wildfire took down that cabin, when they actually burned it on purpose."

Vince said, "We'll just hand this stuff over to Tucker and see what he says."

Jade and Hammer walked up.

"Logan and Tristan are on the helo," Hammer said.

"Hand over what to Tucker?" Jade asked. Vince handed it over, and her eyebrows rose. "Arson."

"Think so," Vince said.

Jade tucked the cigarette butt and the melted earphone into her fire pack. "Okay, let's give this former fire a walk-around. All of us, single file, spaced out. Strong eyes, make sure it's out. Because then we're headed west to meet the bus."

Her head on swivel, Cadee did catch Vince searching intently a few feet away. But he looked pensive. He probably wished he hadn't become a firefighter at this point—wished he was still a DEA fighter for justice so things like this didn't happen.

Maybe next time he would be the innocent left to die.

Cadee wasn't sure she could handle it if that happened.

Sore and tired from the Pulaski work at the fire, Vince had nothing else to think about as they arrived at jump base.

His shoulders weren't actually sore from the hand tool use at the fire. They were sore from the stress, the memories of his DEA work. Those memories were like the embers that had stirred up from the cabin fire and caught the woods around it on fire today.

It was time for him to extinguish the whole DEA thing like they'd extinguished the arson fire.

But Cadee was like fresh air, wind, stirring up love he'd thought had been extinguished.

He needed some space to figure out if he'd even made the right choice sticking with his team rather than going out and proving his innocence.

Thankfully, Logan said he'd take Vince's fire

gear to the men's cabin. Waving at the team, Vince headed out to the west plane hangar.

Also thankfully, it was empty. The plane mechanics had pulled the retardant plane onto the concrete slab in front of it and were working on it, cleaning it, doing regular maintenance, whatever.

With another quick wave he walked into the hanger, turned right. They'd hung Dad's memorial plaque right inside the open hangar door. Somehow, the distant sounds of mechanics, the smells of fresh Alaska air mixing with the smell of jet fuel, the shadowy light, all brought a sense of peace.

Or was it Dad's plaque?

He wished he had Dad to talk to in person. But this solid oak plaque showed what kind of man he'd been. The numbers hurt. Not Dad's birth year. His death year.

It was the rest that mattered, though. "Leader. Inspirer. Motivational force. Teacher. Risk taker. Giver—even of his life. Man of godly character. Man of faith. Cap."

He reached his hand up, ran it over the letters of those words under the engraved portrait of his dad. Skye had drawn the picture that somehow truly caught all those things that described Dad. To the core.

But it was just a picture. He couldn't talk to Dad.

He couldn't talk to God.

He'd think about that, because he needed to straighten it out if he was going to have a relationship with Cadee. And that, he knew he wanted.

First things first though. He could hardly make promises to her when he had no idea what was going to happen.

Vince headed out of the hangar and across the runway to the men's cabin.

Oh. That's what was going to happen.

Two men he didn't know. DEA agents, both of them. Clearly. He would always recognize a DEA agent when he saw a scruffy face absorbing every minute detail around them.

Jade, face red with anger, stood glaring at them. Next to her was Cadee, her fists clenching, unclenching.

She turned, spotted him, came running over. "Vince, where have you been? Everyone is looking for you. They have an arrest warrant."

He nodded. Of course they did.

Hammer jogged up behind Jade and leaned against the porch. Skye sprinted up, tucked into the group. Thankfully the hotshots hadn't come back yet, or this would be chaos.

Vince took a deep breath, strode up. They slid to the side, making a path for him.

The curly-haired agent said, "Hello, Mr. Ramos. I'm Special Agent Davis. DEA." He held out his hand as though it were a friendly welcome.

Vince wasn't going to shake their hands. He could just guess what the DEA was seeing about him—that didn't really exist.

Davis dropped his hand, reached for a piece of paper on the cot and held it out to him. "We do, indeed, have a search warrant. And an arrest warrant. Money laundering. For starters. We'll be adding to it," Davis announced like a judge in court.

Hammer banged the porch rail with his fist.

Skye huffed. "I'm calling Rio," she said. "Hammer, go get Tucker." She raced to the women's cabin, already punching numbers on her phone. Hammer headed to the admin office.

Vince didn't take the paper. And didn't drop eye contact with Davis. The creep had said that on purpose—loudly—so his teammates would hear this manure pile of charges the DEA had come up with.

Davis cleared his throat, dropped the warrant on the top step. "Smith." Pulling a hard-shell black roller bag behind him, he led the bald guy—

Smith apparently—up the stairs into the men's cabin. Steering to Vince's room. Of course.

Except Davis stopped at the door, turned around, narrowed his eyes at Vince, who was at the bottom of the stairs with the group. "You do a lot of wire transfers, Mr. Ramos?"

Cadee scoffed. "Are you kidding—"

Vince caught her eyes, gave her a small smile, a subtle shake of his head. She gave him a nod just as subtle, her lips tightened into a straight line. Jade moved next to Cadee, put her arms around her. "Orion and Tori are still missing. Neil is being treated in the hospital. Now this," she rasped under her breath.

The agents went on into the cabin. Tucker came running up, winked at Vince, and followed the men in while Hammer rejoined the group.

"Commander doesn't want them going through your stuff without an eye on them," Hammer said.

Vince chuckled.

Cadee walked over and stood beside him, her head leaning on his shoulder.

These were federal agents. How could she not believe federal agents?

He looked around at the team. How could anyone not?

Except for those who'd been part of the law enforcement system and so knew that not all of them were perfect.

"Anyway, what's up?" Hammer asked. "What are they looking for?"

"I have an idea, but I don't know for sure. You all heard that they're starting with money laundering."

Jade wrinkled her nose. "You don't even launder your clothes, do you? How could you launder money?"

Everyone chuckled.

Him too. Jade was trying to lighten the mood. It worked. A bit.

Skye walked up, found herself another spot in the group. "Rio, um, can't come tonight," she said. "Sorry about that, Vince."

"No trouble at all." He looked around the group. "You don't have to be here for me. I'll keep you in the circle."

Jade wrinkled her nose. "This is your team. We have your back."

He gulped down the doubt that wanted to rise. "Thanks, Chief."

The DEA agents were led out, or more like marched out, by Tucker down the porch stairs.

Vince felt like his eyes bugged. Davis was pulling that roller bag behind him. It looked heavy. But it had been obviously light when they went up the stairs.

And Smith had a stack of books and papers in his arms. Books he did not recognize.

He wanted to ask what they had found, and he would, but he knew they wouldn't answer, at least not right now.

And he didn't want those answers yet. Not in front of the team. Especially Cadee. He squeezed her in a one-arm hug.

Davis stopped in front of him, stood the roller bag next to himself. "The warrant gives us permission for your phone." He held out his hand.

Vince couldn't stop the warrant. He pulled the phone from his pocket and slapped it into Davis's hand.

But not a word.

"Thank you." His phone went into Davis's pocket. "Turn around."

He wouldn't allow them to force him to the ground.

So he turned.

Smith began to read him his rights. Pulled one arm behind Vince's back. Then the other.

The handcuffs clicked. Tight.

He wanted to punch these DEA jerks.

They could've simply asked him to go with them like a real man. He would've. He was a man of integrity. Like Dad.

He wanted to say all that.

But he bit back the snarl, the sarcasm for these guys.

Definitely not a word.

Davis pointed at the suitcase, the books and papers. "You're not gonna get away with this, Ramos."

TEN

CADEE SAT IN THE CHEAP LAWN CHAIR by the firepit, drinking a strawberry soda.

Waiting for Rio.

She'd been determined to go to the building the DEA was borrowing in Copper Mountain to find out what was happening with Vince after those guys had arrested him, but Skye had said that her husband was on his way.

Her hands curled into fists on the armrests— an attempt to contain her frustration. She knew Vince well enough to know that those handcuffs, the DEA jerks themselves, should never have been here. He was innocent, and anyone could see that.

She wished she could snap her fingers and Rio would materialize though. She'd been waiting for-ty-five—no, forty-seven—minutes for him. She'd been sitting here so long that everyone else had gone to the mess hall to eat while they tried to figure out what was going on.

Cadee wasn't hungry.

Dust flew up from the dirt road as Rio pulled up in an old rusty Jeep. He bumped the curb in the parking lot and drove over, parking in front of the firepit between the cabins. The Jeep gave just a shade of a shudder as he turned it off. He jumped out, and the door squealed as he shut it.

Cadee got up and walked over to him, standing at the firepit. "Rio," she said.

"Cadee." Rio shuffled from foot to foot, then stood tall. "I don't think I can do anything to help him."

Her eyes narrowed. "Really? This is Vince we're talking about."

He tilted his head. "This is the DEA we're talking about."

"Exactly."

His voice flattened. "They don't just make up fake charges, Cadee."

"Before he became a smokejumper, they did. Cleared him. But his coworkers just couldn't stop believing the charges, so he quit that job. And I'm glad he did." She folded her arms across her chest.

"They found new evidence."

"What they found is bull," she yelled. "This is *Vince* we're talking about. *Vince*." She paced around the firepit. How was she going to talk him into doing anything? "Obviously someone planted that evidence."

Rio just calmly leaned against his Jeep, his hands resting in the back pockets of his jeans. "How would they do that? It isn't like people walk onto the jump base off the street. This place is off the beaten path."

She took a deep breath, stopped pacing the firepit, leaned up against the Jeep next to him. "Sorry."

He gave her a gentle smile. "I know." His toe kicked at the dirt. "I know it's Vince. But the DEA has to look at the new evidence, at the new charges. I can't take over a DEA case even if I wanted to—or wasn't in the middle of my own investigation. These militia guys need to be stopped. I need to track down the people who downed your plane and tried to kill you. And more importantly, figure out why."

"I know." She stretched her neck side to side. A breeze gently rustled through the birch trees on the jump base property.

Rio opened his car door, paused, clicked his

tongue. "I can tell you I'll do everything I can for him. Promise." He slid into the car with a wave.

The breeze shifted, and Cadee's eyes automatically scanned the horizon for any smoke. She was glad there wasn't any, because she wanted Vince to get the legal help he needed, deserved. But how was she supposed to do that? She didn't know any lawyers.

Did he have someone there to advocate for him?

Maybe his DEA agent friend was still in town, and he could help.

She wandered to the edge of the property, watching Rio drive away. Trying to figure out how to pray for Vince. She barely knew where to start.

A red sedan headed up the road to the base, kicking up dust behind it. She wandered over to the driver's side, and the guy rolled his window down.

"Nick? Vince's partner, before?"

He smiled. "You must be Cadee—his current partner?"

Had God actually answered her prayer before she'd even figured out what to ask for? "I'm so glad you're here. The DEA just arrested Vince." Saying it aloud brought tears to her eyes.

He gaped. "They did? I was going to say good-bye one more time before I head out."

"Do you know how we can help him?" She prayed he would know what to do.

"Hop in." Nick motioned to his passenger side. "I'm headed to Copper Mountain, so I can drop you off at the DEA office. We can check in on Vince before I go pack up my hotel room."

"Great. That'll save me the gas since you're going that way. I appreciate it, Nick. He'll be glad to see you, I'm sure. Um, just a second." She took out her phone and thumbed a quick text to Jade. She smiled at Nick. "I'm sure my friend will give me a ride home. So yes. I accept."

Cadee slid into the passenger seat. "This is a sharp-looking car. Such soft leather too." She couldn't help saying it. "Good thing I'm not filthy from fighting wildfires." She spent most of her life covered in ash and dirt.

The way it should be.

The way Vince wanted to live his life as well—if she could get him out of this mess.

He laughed, dramatically spread his hands in front of him. "Patagonia red, the agent said when I rented it." He turned the car around on the road. "After driving this rental, I think I'll look into a Mercedes like this when my car lease is up."

Nick left the parking lot and drove to the jump base entry.

She started to text Vince. Grrr. Her phone died. His arrest was on her brain, not charging, well, anything.

"You're quite the texter," Nick said.

She dropped her phone into her lap. She'd have to finish the text to Vince later. Didn't know what to say anyway, or when he'd get to read it. "So, what are you doing up here in Alaska, Nick?"

"A client of mine wants an Alaskan fishing property. He's not the best fisherman, but he does love it, and I can't blame him. This place is full of all kinds of beauty." He glanced at her for a second. He chuckled, then he gestured to her phone sitting in her lap, gave a whistle. "That's an awesome phone. Wish I could afford a swank cell like that . . ." His voice trailed off, green-eyed in tone.

Why would a guy driving a car like this be jealous of her phone?

She grabbed her water bottle and took a long drink. She wasn't wealthy. She'd bought the phone with her savings, instead of buying a much-needed computer, after she'd accidentally lost her old phone in her attempt to save Cap. Raine had grabbed her legs from behind, taking her down to the ground just as she'd reached the fire. The phone had flown out of her pocket and burned up in the fire. Instead of her.

She hadn't been thinking fire at that moment. Only Cap.

But truth was, that fire had been so hot, so strong, that it was a good thing Raine had caught her, or Cadee would likely be dead too.

Nick's gaze slid over to her. "What are the charges against Vince? I haven't heard. Obviously."

Cadee scoffed. "Money laundering. To start with." She shook her head. "I don't buy it. Vince was your DEA partner. You don't believe what they're accusing him of, do you?"

Nick lifted one shoulder, blew out a long, soft breath, grabbed a pack of gum and put a piece in his mouth. He held out the pack to offer her one.

She shook her head.

"This money-laundering thing has taken me by surprise, but I guess in a way I should've seen it coming. Vince's father was on the board of Northern Lights Higher Education Foundation, so . . ." Nick's voice faded. "And I guess you know, but . . ." He sighed. "Vince's mom was arrested for embezzlement."

That wasn't good. Jamie must have seen the

same thing. The DEA had found a bankbook among Vince's things—transactions for the foundation? Who knew what they'd found? How could a former DEA agent even consider Vince's mother's crime to be evidence against Vince? She didn't get it. "I don't see how that means Vince is guilty."

Something just felt off about Nick. Especially when he said, "Maybe the apple didn't fall too far from that tree after all."

Now Cadee wished she hadn't taken a ride with him, but she'd just hear what else he had to say. So she changed the topic. "How do you know Tristan?"

"Who?" Nick glanced at her, then back at the road.

"The guy from Ingriq. You were talking to him."

"Yeah. He's an old California acquaintance. Tristan was an informant for Vince and me during our partner days."

"Oh." Vince had never told her that. Tristan either, though she didn't know him well past the fact he was Jamie's brother. Surely one of them would've acted like they knew each other. Like they'd met before Logan had found Jamie in that militia camp.

Was Nick lying?

Cadee had to say something. "Hate to tell you, but there was a wildfire yesterday. We found him in a burning cabin, and we rescued him."

Nick's head jerked back in surprise. "Oh no. He's still alive?"

"Yes. Your friend is at Providence Hospital in Anchorage. You should make some time to go see him."

She looked over and saw Nick's jaw working. Cadee grabbed her water bottle and sipped at it.

"Was it arson?" Nick asked.

Now Cadee was surprised. Why would that be his first question? But she should keep it simple. "It was. In the middle of a wildfire, someone tried to cover their tracks. Can you believe it?" Far better to sound like a ditzy female than someone quickly figuring out this man was no friend of Vince's.

"Are they looking at Vince for arson? Attempted murder?"

She glugged the rest of her water bottle and stuck the empty in the car's cup holder next to her in the center console. She couldn't just let that go. "Why would you ask that?"

"Vince just seemed to be obsessed with matches and cigarettes . . ." Again with the voice fade. "Back when we were partners. Though I don't want to speak badly about a man I consider my friend."

"But he doesn't smoke, and he's a firefighter."

"I know." He focused on twisting his steel mug in the cup holder and looking out the front window.

This seemed off.

Cadee jiggled her phone in her hand, played with the pop socket.

Vince just seemed to be obsessed with matches and cigarettes.

Yeah, no. She'd never seen them in his possession. Not when they'd been hotshots, nor in smokejumper training. Not on any of their dates. Not fighting fires together with the Midnight Sun crew—even if they did fight each other a lot.

How did Nick even know to mention matches and cigarettes?

Cadee stared at her phone as she silently fidgeted with it.

Wish I could afford a swank cell like that.

This was hardly high value, even if she'd sprung for a non-cheapie phone. Besides, Vince had said Nick was a real-estate agent who traveled through the United States on behalf of wealthy clients—as well as a consultant for the DEA. This was not exactly a guy who couldn't afford an expensive phone.

Tristan was an informant for Vince and me during our partner days.

Vince had been sincere when he'd said it looked like Nick was talking to Tristan during the Ingriq evacuation. Then he'd appraised Nick hard, arms crossed tight. Suspicious. A hundred percent.

Even if he had been his partner.

Vince's mom was arrested for embezzlement.

No way that woman had taught her son how to commit financial crime before her arrest. Nick hadn't said it exactly. But he was former DEA—he knew better.

And no way had Vince skimmed money off the top of the education fund. Hidden the money somehow.

She knew Vince. It wasn't possible.

Every single thing Nick had said kept running through her brain. It all seemed to say one thing . . . and the way Nick's voice consistently trailed off . . .

He had to be leading her to think Vince was guilty. But she *knew* Vince.

Nick was Vince's former DEA partner, yes, but his friend? She wasn't so sure Nick wasn't right in the middle of all this. How, she had no idea. But she couldn't shake the feeling.

What was she doing in the car with him?

She looked over at Nick, drinking coffee from his travel mug. He drove along like normal, weaving to avoid the dirt road's potholes. Nothing suspicious. Except that he'd lied.

Maybe she was wrong and he was just worried about his buddy. Not making sense.

He slipped his mug into the cup holder in front of her empty water bottle. As she studied him, he twisted it around as he drove, one hand on the steering wheel.

Normal guy, right?

Then she saw the highway up ahead. With the turn onto the paved road coming up, Nick touched the brakes, fiddled with the turn signal, flipped it to the left.

Why was he turning toward Ingriq instead of toward Copper Mountain?

He steered the car over, getting ready to make a left turn.

She needed to get out of this car before he hit the road that led to the highway. She wasn't getting on the highway with this guy.

God!

Suddenly her gut knew exactly what to do.

Cadee pointed out his side of the car, shrieked. "Watch out!"

He glanced out the window, decelerating hard.

Perfect. She grabbed the steering wheel. Tried to steer the car off the road.

"What are you doing?" he screamed, pulling the steering wheel the other way.

They fought over control of the steering wheel. The car kicked up dust and swerved side to side across the road.

"What are you doing?" he yelled again.

She twisted and reached her right hand over to the steering wheel. With her left, she knocked his right hand off the wheel. She pulled hard with her left hand as his foot stayed on the brake, and the car rolled into the ditch.

Cadee shoved the door open and jumped out. She ran up the embankment, scrambling to the top so she could race into the trees and lose him.

Gunshots whizzed past her.

She sprinted across the road and jumped over the ditch, diving into the mass of salmonberry bushes beside the ditch.

Again.

How was she going to help Vince now?

Vince sat at the counter-height table in the Copper Mountain meeting room being used by the DEA. Davis and Smith stood across the table from him, took turns throwing questions at him. Ones that he refused to answer. He wasn't just sitting there quietly. He was sitting there in passive-aggressive silence. This was nuts. These two men were nuts.

Skye's husband Rio threw open the door. A DEA no-name spun and blocked him from coming in. "Who are you?" he demanded.

"Rio Parker, FBI." He showed his badge as he surveyed the DEA guy's badge. "Hello, Smith. How are you gentlemen today?"

Davis turned to face Rio. "We'll be done with Mr. Ramos in a while."

Rio pushed past Smith, slid into the seat next to Vince. "I don't take cases away from a friendly federal agency, but I decided I couldn't ignore this interesting case," he said. He thumped Vince's shoulder. "If that's okay with you?"

Vince smiled, gave him a nod. About time someone was on his side.

Rio held out his hand to the DEA creeps. "May I please see the warrant?"

Davis rolled his eyes, handed him the paperwork. "Professional courtesy," he mumbled.

Rio scanned over the document. "Embezzlement from Northern Lights Higher Education Foundation."

"We're turning it over to the Secret Service. Ramos is facing one to three years," Davis said with a smirk. "Unless he wants to help us take down the militia. We found anhydrous ammonia and a case of cough syrup among Mr. Ramos's things in the Midnight Sun men's cabin."

Rio looked up. "You want to add charges on the chemical processing."

Davis kept talking. "What we find is what we find. We were trying to take down this militia after meth dealing led us to them. Turns out we found chemical processing instead. We were looking into their financials when we found they were skimming from the Northern Lights Higher Education Foundation. Since Vince's dad was on the board, we wanted to talk to Vince himself. He wouldn't respond to our messages."

Rio's eye twitched. "What do you mean?"

Clearly proud of himself, Davis reached for a tablet, made a few clicks, slid it across the table. "These are copies of Vince's bankbook and property paperwork. The total of that missing money from NLHE Foundation is exactly what was spent on the real estate he bought in the areas the militia were operating in. Clearly worthy of the warrant."

Rio scanned through the documents in the silence that settled. Then he tilted his head. "So an informant led you to the NLHE Foundation and the money laundering?"

"No. We don't have an informant involved." Davis opened his mouth, then shut it. He looked out the window for a long moment.

"Well?" Rio asked.

Davis's hyper-confidence fell a couple percent. "Yesterday morning, the physical bankbook and property paperwork were dropped off at our office. Anonymously."

Rio said, "So you have no idea where they came from or if they're legit."

Davis cleared his throat, straightened in his seat. "If Ramos cooperates with us, we'll drop the chem charge and the money-laundering charges. But we can't drop the forfeiture of his property."

"What property do I even have?" Vince said under his breath.

Davis kept going. "Or the attempted murder charges we will be filing for events that have recently come to our attention."

Rio's eyes closed.

A drip of cold sweat snaked down Vince's spine.

Rio calmly set the tablet aside. "Explain that, Davis."

"Nick Atwood, former DEA agent, told us last night he was shot at. Vince's gun is the same caliber. Clearly they had a beef, and Vince took the opportunity to try and kill his former partner."

Rio glanced at Vince.

Vince just shook his head. He could have anyone at the jump base verify he'd been there last night, not out in the backcountry trying to kill Nick. "I have a forty-five that belonged to my father. It's in the gun safe in Hammer's room, which these guys didn't touch. That is the only gun I know of."

Rio said, "And which they won't be getting a warrant for."

Davis didn't seem to care much about the particulars. He continued, "Now we have the additional arson charge we can add to the attempted murder charge."

"That won't stick," Rio said. "On a guy who doesn't smoke? What is 'Vince's brand' anyway?" He finger-quoted the words.

Still, the truth sank into Vince. This was all about Jamie's brother.

What had Tristan been doing talking to Nick in Ingriq during the evacuation? Surely Rio knew what connected Tristan to the militia. Vince just needed to get the guy alone.

Rio tapped on the tablet, then leaned forward, slid the tablet back across the table. "Emailed myself the copies of the documents. I'm sure you got a picture of the anonymous person who delivered the evidence. Show me."

Davis pulled up the picture and gave back the tablet. Rio tilted it so Vince could see.

Landon. Vince's eyes widened, and Rio gave him a nod. "This man is under arrest, connected to the militia."

Finally, they were getting somewhere.

Rio slid the tablet back to Davis. "Thanks, I emailed that image to myself as well. Anyway, I took a look into Mr. Ramos's financials, along with a consultant of mine, and we have proof he is not connected to the California real-estate purchase. In fact, his only crime is having an account at the same bank." He glanced at Vince. "Seriously, their rates are criminal. There are better banks in Alaska."

Vince tried not to laugh. But couldn't help it.

Rio winked at him, then speared Davis with his

gaze. "This is neither his habit nor his personality. Nor is murder. This is not going to work for you."

Davis tapped his chin for a second, then signaled to his colleague. The two of them whispered to each other for a good couple of minutes.

Vince's stomach twisted even further as they waited.

Davis finally nodded, turned to Rio. "So you're here to work with us, Parker?" Davis asked Rio. "We could use the FBI's support on this. We've been wanting to take down this militia for a few months. You can talk Ramos here into cooperating."

"Good luck with that." Vince folded his arms.

After they'd pulled this stunt? No way was he gonna help them.

"Tell you what," Rio said, turning on the charm he'd been famous for as an undercover. "Vince might be a former DEA agent, but he's choosing not to talk to you. I have a relationship with the Midnight Sun firefighters. He'll talk to me. If you want him to talk at all, you better let me do it."

Vince kept his humor to himself. Rio certainly knew how these guys operated—he'd pegged them perfectly.

Davis stepped back, leaned against the opposite wall next to his colleague.

Rio's fingers tapped the table as he looked between the two.

Davis rolled his eyes. "Fine, fine." He pushed up from the wall, and the two DEA agents walked out. Left the door open.

Rio chuckled, got up and closed the door behind them. "Those guys are a piece of work."

"Listen, Rio—"

Rio held up his hand. "Hold up and let me go first. I need to apologize. Skye tried to get me to come. Cadee too. Skye's mad enough I may have to sleep on the couch tonight. That's okay. I explained to both of them—specifically Cadee— why I couldn't be here to help you. This is a DEA job, and I've not been assigned to work with them on it."

"You said that to her?" He couldn't imagine how Cadee had responded to that.

"By the time I got home from the jump base and made myself a sandwich for lunch, I'd had some thinking time. I knew I should be here. So, sorry."

Vince gulped. "Thanks."

"Problem is," Rio said, "no matter how well we know someone, they might be guilty." He pointed at the tablet. "The bankbook and property documents are what gave them the warrant." He waved his hands in the air. "They obviously found other evidence. So I want to hear you out." He stepped into Vince's space. "Everything. Got it?"

He'd seen Rio at almost all the Midnight Sun picnics. Skye's husband. Good guy. Detective skills. If he was going to talk to anyone, this was who he'd pick.

He took a second to sort through everything in his head. "That guy in the picture? That's Landon. He shot at Cadee and me, but he missed. We used a shortcut and surprised him, caught him. The Ingriq AST department took him into custody."

"I'd love to hear that full story sometime." Rio made a note on a paper. "I'll follow up on that."

Vince's smile lasted half a second. "I'll tell you at the next Midnight Sun picnic. Anyway, we zip-tied him and walked him into Ingriq Village. Cadee's..." He couldn't say ex. Just couldn't. "Cadee's buddy, Jared Jensen, is a trooper. He recognized Landon as part of the militia, took him into custody."

"I'll get in touch with him."

"My guess is Landon was with the rest of the militia that shot at us earlier."

"Huh." Rio was scribbling notes.

"I carried that brand of cigarettes. Once. In a DEA undercover thing. I do not smoke."

Rio's lips twisted. "All right, then." He chuckled. "I didn't think you did."

"All I can say about the chem processing is that I never purchased either ammonia or cough syrup. Maybe one bottle of cough syrup last year. Don't remember what brand." The fact he even had to say that, to fight for his innocence, was enough to make him go crazy.

Rio rubbed his chin in thought.

"And that bankbook, the foundation ledger. It looks like it's from my bank, but I use the Bankbook Online app. That way I can check my account, pay my bills and whatever, even at the jump base."

"Kids have fake social accounts all the time so their parents can't see what they're doing. Do you have an online bank account that looks good, and a physical ledger to keep track of what you're really doing?"

"No."

"Wire transfers, property money laundering, chemical processing. Clearly, the DEA believes you are in deep with the militia, and they aren't going to let that idea go easily. The attempts on Winters and Atwood . . ." He scratched the back of his head. "To stop them from tattling, maybe."

The muscles in the back of Vince's neck were so

taut that a headache took over. "That only means *they're* connected, not me."

Rio leaned forward into his space. "How do you know Tristan Winters?"

"I don't. He's Jamie's brother, so Logan knows him." The guy had been on the plane with them when it crashed. Why did that seem like so long ago when it was only yesterday? "I saw him talking to Nick when Cadee and I were in the village helping with the evacuation. I didn't even talk to him then."

Rio narrowed his eyes.

"And I don't have a gun except my father's."

Rio shrugged. "You could've used someone else's gun. Maybe Winters was one of your informants from your DEA time."

"Pretty sure I would've remembered the guy if he was."

"Here's what I need to know." He pointed straight at Vince's heart. "Why did you try to kill Winters? And Atwood?"

Vince felt the blood rush from his face. "You know me better than that, Rio. I have zero reason to do it, and others can corroborate my whereabouts at the time of the supposed shooting."

"And what about the Higher Ed money? Are you on the board?"

"No. My dad was. They've asked me—that's all. I have no idea what that is about."

"Okay." Rio tilted his head to the left, then straightened the papers on the table into a perfect rectangle. "All right, I believe you, Vince. So you've convinced at least me. I just have one thing to say . . . this is all kinds of coincidental."

If he had Rio on his side, it was only a matter of time before he convinced everyone else. "I have no idea what's happening here."

"Whatever it is, you're in the middle of it." Rio stood. "I'll talk to the DEA. Hopefully I can get you released so you can get back to work. And hire yourself an attorney."

ELEVEN

THIS WAS THE STUPID THIRD TIME she'd been shot at. Third time!

Cadee hunkered down in yet another stupid mass of salmonberry bushes. *Again.* Fine, she was scared. But it was far better to be angry than overwhelmed by fear.

It was just that the stupid DEA guys had somehow decided to arrest Vince. And there was that stupid real-estate money-laundering charge—which didn't even make sense when he rented his house.

And that stupid Rio, who'd refused to go back him up.

No. She was the most stupid of all. She'd agreed to take a ride from Nick in that stupid Patagonia-red stupid Mercedes.

Cadee sighed.

Fact was, God had created her with a sense of adventure, and that sometimes meant leaping the roadside ditch and landing in stu—in thorny bushes.

She huffed as she gently rubbed at the scratches all over her arm.

God, I need to get back to the jump base.

But she hadn't dared to move as Nick crashed around a bit, walked a ways up and down the road, looking for her.

Suddenly, Nick yelled out, "All right, Cadee. I'll be back for you."

He started his car, backed it out of the shallow ditch she'd driven it into.

She could hear the fading of the engine but stayed hidden until she was sure he was completely gone. She gently moved her arm away from the thorns, then slowly moved the salmonberry branches aside so she could see out to the road.

She couldn't see the sedan.

Cadee took a deep breath and crawled carefully, but painfully, under the salmonberry bushes and away from the road. When she hit the other edge of the mass of bushes, she finally stood.

Better this than trusting Nick like Vince did. Look where that'd gotten him—under arrest.

Stop that. The men had been partners. No wonder he trusted Nick. The man had been seriously convincing. If he hadn't tried to tell her they knew Tristan from their DEA days, she might've believed him.

She reached into her pocket for her phone to call Vince. Wrong pocket. She patted every single pocket. Oh yeah, it had been on her lap in Nick's sedan. Cadee looked all around, under the bushes. Great. No phone. It must have fallen into the car when she'd jumped out. Of course.

She twisted around her tracker ring, wishing the ring had a feature to send the team an alert.

Show me what to do, Lord. I—I'm not sure what to do.

She couldn't use the road, in case Nick was waiting somewhere to trap her. She looked left and right down the highway in front of her, turned and checked the dirt road to the base.

No Mercedes that she could see, but a woodpecker sat most of the way up a spruce tree, tapping at the trunk like it was a drum. There was a pretty strong wind blowing the sedges and grasses that filled the flat, empty land. But it didn't matter.

She knew what to do.

She started jogging to base. She would run just

inside the bushes and jump back into the salmonberries if necessary. Her lips pursed. Only *if* necessary. After all, she was already scratched up and bleeding.

Forty-five minutes later, Cadee arrived at the jump base.

She stopped with her hands on her hips and looked around, breathing hard. She saw lights on in the mess hall and sprinted across the runway, praying everyone was in there and not in the cabins. She raced in and the door slammed closed behind her.

Vince spun around. "Cadee, are you okay?"

She tried to speak, but all she could do was breathe hard from running so far.

He stepped into her space, pulled her into a hug. She sank into his arms, resting in his hold. Her breath hitched in her throat, but she refused to cry even though her eyes stung. "I'm okay."

He didn't let her go.

"I'm not lying."

Vince chuckled and rubbed his hand up and down her back. "I'll give you a second. Then you can tell me if you need to see the medic." He grabbed her hands in his.

The rest of the team gathered around. When he finally let her go, Cadee ran her hands through her hair, working through the tangles. Leaves and twigs from when she'd been hiding under the bushes dropped to the ground.

"What happened?" Logan urged, and Skye dittoed him, her phone already out to call Rio.

Cadee's throat constricted. She stepped back, overwhelmed by the force of their care for her. They were really worried. Her hands fidgeted in Vince's.

"What is it?" Vince asked.

She tried to take another step back, but he didn't let go of her hands. "I . . . I'm sorry."

"Come on, Cadee," he said. "Tell me why you're all scratched up."

She sniffed. "Nick shot at me."

He dropped her hands. "What?"

"He said he would give me a ride to the DEA office to be there for you."

Vince smiled. "Rio handled things, so I'm here." Then he frowned as he looked at the scratches on her arms, her cheeks. "Tell me."

"Nick kidnapped me. I jumped out of his sedan, and he shot at me." Her eyes watered.

Skye headed for the door, pushing numbers into her phone as she strode out.

Cadee knew she owed Vince, the team, the whole story.

Hammer handed her a much-needed bottle of water, put his hand on her back, and guided them all to one of the tables. "Let me see your arms."

She sat, and he held her wrist gently, easing her arm over to see underneath. He dropped her hand in her lap and stood. "I'll be back."

Vince tipped up his chin, his eyebrows furrowed. "Surely Nick saw a moose or a bear and wanted to keep them away from you."

"I saw no evidence of animals in the area, Vince, and that bullet went right past me."

Vince shifted in his seat. "Why would he do that?"

"He thought the DEA must be right about your money-laundering charges. I didn't agree."

"Are you sure?" asked Vince.

She nodded as she drained the water, wiped her mouth. "Yes. One hundred percent. He implied the new charges against you were because your dad was on the Northern Lights board. Dumb!" She looked down to the floor. "And because your mom committed embezzlement. Sorry."

His lips twisted.

"Nick also implied you must have tried to kill Tristan, given the arson with cigarettes and matches."

Vince looked out the window, his jaw worked. "He still has contacts in the DEA."

Rio and Jared walked in with Skye. She took a seat, but the two law enforcement guys just stood. Vince was glad to see Rio, and even the trooper.

"How did he even know about the cigarettes and matches?" Rio asked.

She looked up into his face. "Honestly, no clue whatsoever. I told him about his buddy, Tristan. I thought he'd like to stop and see him at the hospital in Anchorage, but he just started talking about the cigarettes and matches." She glanced over at Vince. "Nick said that was your brand of cigarettes."

He chuckled, and Cadee suddenly realized he was still holding her hand. Rio grinned. "Thanks to a follow-up with the DEA, we now know that Vince carried a pack of that brand. Once. On an undercover job."

Jade spoke up. "Not during his SJ job."

Cadee didn't need them to back him up on that. "He never smoked once while we dated."

Jade glanced between them. "You guys were a thing?"

How could she even answer that? She bit her lip.

"Never mind, that actually kind of explains a lot."

Rio leaned in, his fists on the table. "Anyway . . ."

Thanks for changing the topic, Rio.

He pinned her gaze with his. "Why'd you jump out of the car, Cadee?"

Oh. That new topic. She sucked in a shaky breath. "We were almost to the highway when he flipped his turn signal to head toward the village instead of to Wasilla and Anchorage. He'd already lied about you knowing Tristan."

Vince nodded. "The DEA said the same to me."

"I distracted him. We fought over the steering wheel, but I was able to steer the Mercedes into the ditch. I jumped out, and when he shot at me, I dove into the salmonberry bushes on the other side of the road. I hid until he finally decided to back his car out of the ditch and leave. I waited even longer, then jogged here. Kept the bushes between me and the road in case."

Vince leaned over and kissed her forehead. "You did the right thing. Just wish you would've called us."

"After the whole thing in Nick's car, I couldn't find my phone."

He squeezed her hand. "We'll help you look where you jumped out tomorrow."

Hammer came back with a handful of medical supplies and sat by her. He put cream on her scratches and started unwrapping a stack of tiny bandages.

Vince stood. "Rio, are you going to look at Nick or what?"

"Absolutely. We still need to sort through the evidence the DEA has against you. But he will definitely be charged with attempting to murder Cadee." He stuffed his hands into his pockets, looked over at her. "You willing to testify?"

She snorted. "One hundred percent."

"Okay, getting a call in to my partner." Rio walked over to Skye and pecked his wife on the cheek, then strolled out of the room.

Vince sat down and grabbed Cadee's hand again. The one Hammer had finished patching up. He looked at her injuries for a long moment.

Cadee said, "I'm okay."

Vince just kissed her forehead again.

Jade leaned back in her seat and locked her hands behind her head. The movement caught Cadee's gaze. Had her eyebrows just bobbed up and down? Jade mouthed the word *together* and grinned. "Things should be more peaceful now, I'm thinking."

Cadee shook her head. Vince chuckled. She looked around the table, where each person present suddenly had to take a drink, look out the window, or peruse the bulletin board.

Maybe she should pull back the hand Vince was holding, since the rest of the team—

"I'm done." Hammer scooped up the trash and stood.

"Hey, Cadee, you know a good local attorney? I need one."

She squeezed Vince's hand. "We'll find you someone."

Jade slapped her thighs and stood. "All's well that ends well and all that. Get some sleep tonight, everyone. We're deploying to the Hurricane Turn fire at first light." She slipped out.

Vince stood and tugged Cadee up from her seat. They left the mess hall and headed toward the women's cabin.

He wrapped his arm around her as they walked. "You know, you scared me today."

"I scared myself." She laughed.

"Are you kidding? No way. You handled yourself more than capably. I'm so glad you're not hurt."

"Aw, thanks." She squeezed his hand.

Then they stood at the bottom of the stairs in front of the cabin. Vince kicked at the gravel like some awkward teenage boy. Which he wasn't. He turned in front of her, taking both of her hands in his. "I . . . well, I'll see you tomorrow."

She smiled. "See you tomorrow, Vince."

Parachuting down to the wildfire along the Talkeetna–Hurricane Turn railroad, Vince enjoyed the peaceful quiet.

Yesterday, after the DEA warrant and Rio's questioning, Vince had thought he was back with the team and that Cadee would be at the jump base. But no one had known where she was.

He'd been about to use the tracker ring app to find her when she'd come in the doors.

Bleeding and freaked out.

She was a tough woman—tougher than he'd even known. True, things between them weren't fixed. Yet. But they were looking up. In front of the women's cabin last night . . . He knew what he'd almost said, which he wasn't ready for.

Yet.

The quiet of the parachute ride down was definitely about to end. The area was already covered in smoke, and he could hardly see their landing zone. The fire was widespread along the Hurricane Turn railroad, and they were being dropped near Hurricane Gulch Bridge that soared over Hurricane Creek.

Because of the people and families who really wanted to live alone and chose isolation, and for whom the flag-stop train was their main resource, they were going to make sure the fire didn't cause damage to that bridge.

He'd ridden the train with Logan just for fun last month.

Maybe he and Cadee . . .

He focused on his steering lines as he came down in the open spot near the bridge, and Hurricane Creek rumbled gently three hundred feet below. He landed beside Cadee but concentrated on wrapping up his parachute as quickly as possible.

Thinking of the DEA and Nick, Vince was ready to dig into the fire line just to work out his frustration. His Pulaski felt good in his hands, his axe by his side. With the DEA and Nick at the top of his thoughts, he could put down this fire by himself.

He chuckled under his breath. Funny how he'd trusted his DEA teammates and that'd failed. But this Midnight Sun team, they were trustworthy. They had integrity, and they had his back.

His chest tightened as he remembered confronting Cadee after his father's funeral. *You don't care about my father, I don't care about you. We're done.* What kind of guy was he?

They had to talk later. After the DEA pile of manure was dealt with.

If she'd listen to him.

I owe her a real apology, Jesus, not just a "sorry I blamed you for Dad's death."

Wait, had he just actually prayed?

He didn't pair up with anyone as they headed to the bridge. He silently fell in at the end of the line behind Jade.

They reached the spot near the bridge and gathered. Jade looked over at Cadee. "We need you as spotter—on the bridge, the anchorage section, not in the middle of it."

"You got it, Chief," Cadee called. She'd moved well all morning despite the abrasions on her arms. Hammer had bandaged them to keep everything clean while they worked, and then he'd gone out with the hotshots to work a fire closer to where a couple of hikers had said they thought they'd seen Orion and Tori.

Something else he could pray about. Later.

"Skye, you and Logan cut line from the anchor point of the bridge out. Vince, you and I will cut line from the end of the fire to the bridge."

Skye gave her a silly military salute, while Logan called, "Yes, Chief."

And they all took off to their assigned positions.

Jade jogged backward in front of Vince, shouting so the others could hear her, "Be careful, everyone. There is a ton of loose gravel." She turned back around and slid just a bit before she caught her balance. She laughed. "See what I mean?"

Vince chuckled. "You're about as stable as that plane we deployed in."

"The loaner from Boise?" She rolled her eyes. "I hope they get us a new one soon. But I think they're worried about us crashing it again. As if."

They got to the edge of the fire. "How did this fire get to be a long line along the railroad like this?"

Jade shrugged, dug her Pulaski into the ground. "Who knows? At least we're preventing it from getting to the bridge or spreading out into the woods behind us."

He took a step to extend the fire line, and the rocks under his feet slipped. He did what he had to and avoided landing on the ground.

Jade laughed. "That's a great two-step dance you've got there, Vince." She would've been rolling on the ground laughing at him—if she weren't busy with her McLeod.

He joined in. Because . . . yeah. That'd happened.

He focused back on his Pulaski, and he and Jade silently found a rhythm. They could hear Logan's and Skye's hand tools a few hundred feet away.

From the bridge, Cadee's voice split the air. "The wind is shifting. Crown fire is starting."

Vince and Jade stopped in unison, tipped their heads up to survey the fire situation.

"Above you, Skye!" Cadee screamed.

Skye and Logan scrambled out from under the tree, slapping at embers that wanted to land on them. Skye ended up on her face thanks to the rocks and gravel. Logan grabbed her under the armpit and hauled her up.

Jade pointed at them. "You know the crown fire rule . . ."

"Run like the devil's chasing you," Logan shouted.

They all scrambled back toward the safety line, their rendezvous spot if anything kicked off. Vince heard a crash behind him. A burning spruce limb had caught Logan behind it. Logan was smacking at a small fire on his upper arm. Jade and Skye came up behind him and used their shovels to put out the spruce limb while Vince used his Pulaski to clear the floor litter before the fire spread farther.

Then it was out, and they all raced to the safety line.

Skye and Logan started arguing over whether she needed to look at the spot where the fire had burned his arm.

Vince chuckled, took out yet another bottle of water from his fire pack. Stay hydrated, right?

He'd expected Cadee to get to the safety line too. She'd been a little farther than they were, but where was she? Still on her way, hopefully. He looked around, didn't see her, and backed up as a group of moose ran past, fleeing the danger.

Over by the bridge, Cadee screamed.

Vince flinched, but he couldn't run yet. A final moose came racing past with its awkward legs, trying to catch up with the rest of the small herd.

"Checking on Cadee," he called.

"This is a crown fire, Vince. Let me get the plane to dump a slurry. She's probably on her way to the safety zone, at any rate." Jade fixed him with her gaze.

He stared back at her. This was Cadee they were talking about.

"Crown fires move fast. Especially up a hill. You know this."

Vince looked down at his feet for a long moment, looked up the hill covered with towering spruce trees. The fire didn't look good. Jade was right about the slurry. "Sorry, Chief."

He jogged over to the bridge. Where was she?

"Cadee!" he called out.

Nothing. He heard nothing, just the sound of the water, the roar of the fire.

He pulled out his phone and looked at the tracker ring app, clicked on her name.

He turned around. It said she was on the bridge. But she wasn't. The bridge was an iron lattice almost three hundred feet above Hurricane Creek and almost a thousand feet long. She couldn't have just disappeared.

His blood turned to ice. He went up to the where the bridge met the land and looked down.

Cadee lay on a narrow ledge of rock.

Blood dripping from her face.

TWELVE

DON'T MOVE, CADEE. *DON'T MOVE!"*
Vince yelled. "Be back. Give me a minute."

She could breathe. Vince had found her.
Then his footsteps faded.

Cadee sat up . . . carefully. She was on a ledge
below the bridge anchorage. Not like she could
reach the bridgework from here. Or even the anchorage.

That awkward, confused moose calf chasing
after the rest of its group had managed to knock
her down here. She was fine. Fine. She just did
not want to fall three hundred feet into Hurricane Creek. She wiped the sweat from the side
of her head.

Wait. She looked down at her hand. That was
blood. She wiped again. Whatever. She hadn't

gone unconscious or anything. She needed to get out of here, help her team. This was a crown fire, and she wanted to be part of the fight against it.

She stood and tried to reach up to the bridge. She could pull herself up like she had on the tree she'd parachuted into after the plane crash. She reached for it, but it was absolutely too far.

The ledge she'd landed on wasn't too far down from the top, but it was scary high. *Thanks for not letting me dive into Hurricane Creek, God.*

She twisted and looked for fingerholds and toeholds in the rock wall. Yeah, she could do this.

Carefully.

Her head spun and she sank back down. She wrapped her hands around her head. This was all she could handle in prayer right now.

Suddenly, she heard several footsteps running to the bridge.

"Took a few to get a rope and a harness."

She looked up into Vince's face, and her head suddenly wasn't spinning.

Then Jade popped her head over. "Sorry it took so long. They got the rope harness set up while I called for a slurry drop. The hero we call Vince refused to wait for all of us to come get you."

"Sorry, Chief," Vince said. "This is Cadee we're talking about, and I just . . ."

She heard Vince but couldn't make out the rest of the sentence because her thoughts were bubbling. Vince had come to find *her*.

The plane flew over, this time dropping red fire-retardant slurry over where she had seen the start of the crown flames.

Meanwhile, the team dropped the halter at the end of the rope down to her.

Vince leaned over the bridge. "We got you." His voice sounded as worried as the deep frown on his face made him look.

She chuckled and slowly, carefully put on the halter. "I'm ready."

"Let's pull her up," Jade called.

"We've got you, Cadee!" Skye yelled.

She started to rise alongside the rock wall in the diamond shadows of the bridge's girders. The sound of the fire was the background to the grunts and groans. Logan's hands pulled her over the lip and plopped her onto the ground. He plopped next to her . . . and the rest of the team.

Cadee couldn't help but chuckle. "Panting? Really? All those grunts, those groans? You guys better get yourselves into the gym from now on."

Logan started to say something. Vince threw dirt at him. "Don't even think about it, buddy."

"I said nothing." Logan lifted both hands.

Vince laughed. "Hey, Skye, you need to look at this girl's head."

"Got my Kestrel?" Jade asked.

Cadee's face heated up as she stood up and took off the halter set-up. "No, it dropped into the creek. I'm so sorry."

She shrugged. "Just put the halter back on. We'll get a longer rope—much longer—and lower you down to the creek to get it for me."

"Really?" Cadee said, then realized her boss was teasing her. Jade grinned at her, gently pushed her—like she pushed her to be a better firefighter. Every day.

Skye nudged her. "Sit down. Let me look at that head cut."

She eased down onto a boulder.

Jade said, "Okay. We got Cadee back, and she's on break now." She looked at Logan's arm with a scowl.

"Skye wrapped it up, see?" He held up the arm with a frown. "Wasn't much of a burn anyway."

"Okay, fine. Logan and Vince, we're going to go finish that fire line. Even if I don't know the weather stats."

"What happened?" Skye touched Cadee's cheeks, focused on the wound.

"I think the moose's antler caught me. He was a mess. Seemed lost."

Skye chuckled, looked in her eyes for a concussion. "That moose calf didn't end up lost though. She was chasing after the rest of the group when we saw them." Then she poured some water on a gauze square and pressed it against Cadee's wound.

"Did you see what Jade found while clearing the fire line?"

"No."

"A flame thrower."

"Wow. That's how this fire started?"

"I know, right?" Skye's fingers probed the wound. "All right. Looks like it's just a bit of a deep cut." She took a thick gauze square from her first aid kit and taped it in place.

"Yeah. Thanks, Skye."

"No problem. Let's go fight that fire, girl. Just no crazy for you, okay? Stay hydrated, of course."

If that's what it took to join the fire fight. "I promise."

They stood up, but that's when the other three came jogging back.

"Kestrel or no, one thing is obvious," Jade announced. "The wind shifted and drove the fire into our line, so it's only a matter of time before it burns itself out. Good work everyone. The chopper is ready to pick us up whenever we're done doing mop-up. Meanwhile, let's take a break." She brought out granola bars from the toolbox.

Vince sat down beside Cadee, and she leaned against his shoulder.

Jade came up to him with a granola bar. He reached out, but she kept hold of it.

Vince knew what that meant. "Waiting to work *together* to get Cadee out of this mess is what I should've done. Sorry, Chief. In the future . . ."

"Hmmm," Jade rumbled. She looked back and forth between Vince and Cadee. "Okay. This time."

"It won't happen again, Chief."

She passed over both granola bars in her hand and walked over to where Logan had finally given in to Skye's demand to take a rest, considering he was technically still recovering from the hit on the head.

Cadee stepped into Vince's arms, leaned her head on his shoulder. "Thanks for coming after me."

"You should know by now I always will."

Of course she knew he always would. She shifted, looked up into those rich, dark eyes of his.

One hand resting on her neck, Vince drew her to himself, pressed his lips against hers.

He tilted his head, grinning. "I've so missed—"

Cadee moved close to him again, lifted her face to his, her arms resting around his broad shoulders. His arms found the perfect spot around her waist.

And they kissed. Again.

Then there was the clapping.

Oh yeah. Everyone could see them. Laughing, she buried her head in Vince's shoulder.

But man, that was a kiss that would keep her warm in an Alaskan winter.

Back at the jump base, Vince hoped he and Cadee could take a separate table in the mess hall. They needed to talk.

Except she said, "See ya. Need a shower." And walked toward the women's cabin.

After that kiss?

She stopped, looked back. "I mean, we do need to talk." She shifted from foot to foot. Almost took a step forward. "But I also need to figure out how to get a shower and some aspirin."

He nodded. She waved and headed into her cabin.

Well, that was that. He did need to think about something other than Cadee and the kiss and the hand holding.

Besides, the granola bar had barely been a tide-over snack.

He went into the mess hall, dropping his flight bag with the others in the entryway. The rest of the team sat at a table, drinking coffee and sharing a tray heavily loaded with crackers, cheese, meat, nuts, and veggies.

He walked up to the coffee station to the side of the group and filled his mug.

". . . the cigarette pack minus a cigarette in his bag—that matched the butt from the cabin," Logan said. He threw a slice of cucumber into his mouth. "And there were chem processing ingredients under his cot."

Some coffee spilled over Vince's mug, nearly burning his fingers. They were talking about *his* bag.

Jade cleared her throat loudly, jerking her head toward Vince.

Red flamed up Logan's neck. "Um, sorry, Vince. I was just filling them in. I didn't mean . . ."

Vince worked his jaw, dumped some of the coffee out of the mug so it wasn't overfilled, screwed on the lid, and left it sitting at the coffee station.

He stepped up to Logan. "As an FBI agent, Rio is a very competent man focused on truth. Unlike those two DEA agents. When Rio and I were talking, he mentioned how all those things from my space were—and I quote—'all kinds of coincidental.'"

Logan kept talking. "It's just that the DEA agents aren't incompetent or anything—"

Vince took another step toward Logan.

Jade's chair scraped as she stood, glaring at Logan and ready to move between them.

Then Logan's chin dipped.

Vince could've counted twenty heartbeats in the tense silence.

"I wasn't thinking...coincidental is right. You don't smoke. Not even an idiot would hide anhydrous ammonia and a *case* of cough syrup under a cot in a firefighter dorm. Sorry." He held out a hand with a grin. "Besides, Rio clearly got you let loose from that arrest."

Vince took a deep breath to let it all go, and they shook hands. To be fair, the whole thing was weird.

Logan pulled up a chair for him. Vince smiled a thank-you and joined the group.

Skye was tapping her hand on the table while she took a sip of coffee. "Of course, Rio's right.

Coincidental. Problem is that bankbook and those property papers. They seem real even if the accounts aren't." She grimaced. "Sorry, Vince. Didn't mean anything."

Vince grabbed some crackers and some of each kind of cheese. "I know. No offense taken. Thing is, those wire transfers and my signature on the real-estate papers will be harder to disprove. It looks like I'm affiliated with the militia when I own property where they operate. No wonder the DEA jerks were digging into me. And . . ." His stomach twisted, but he ordered it to get in line. He looked around the group. "That's why they so easily added attempted murder charges. Or will add them soon."

Skye's jaw dropped.

Jade's face furrowed into a frown.

Logan shook his head slowly back and forth.

Were any of them going to talk?

Vince said, "When the cops ask you guys about my whereabouts the other night, just tell them what you know."

Logan got a look of certainty on his face. "You're not a murderer."

"Tell the truth, bro."

"Right." Jade clapped her hands in front of her. "This is going to sound random, but I'm hoping it isn't. I looked in our supplies and saw that flame thrower I found at the wildfire was missing from *our* equipment. I loaded it into the box and now it's gone."

"That's weird all right," Skye muttered.

Logan clicked his tongue. "How could you have tried to kill Nick when you were here with us? That is what you're talking about, isn't it?"

"They figure you guys are covering my backside. So said Davis." He shuddered. "Guy just doesn't sit right with me."

Furrows took over Jade's face again. "Of course we would cover your backside. But not in a criminal protection kind of way."

"Of course. Which is why we *are* covering your back." Logan play-punched Vince's shoulder.

"Thanks, everyone."

Skye held up one finger after another. "Bankbook, property purchase paperwork, chem processing stuff, cigarette pack. The question is, how did those things get in Vince's stuff?"

Vince had never heard this high-energy, high-tease group quiet for more than two seconds at a time.

Nick had been in Ingriq during the evacuation. It was totally possible that he'd been here on the base for some reason when Cadee left for Copper

Mountain. Vince would like to hear exactly what she and Nick had talked about on that ride.

He sprang out of his seat. "Hey, Logan, would you ask Jamie to look into that bankbook? And the property purchase." Then he headed out to find Cadee.

Vince arrived at the women's cabin just as Raine was walking out. "Cadee in there?" he asked.

"Nope. She was headed out to have dinner and watch a movie at Emma's, in celebration of the end of the Ingriq fire. Wish I could have home-made chicken noodle soup."

"Thanks." He'd grab her first thing at breakfast.

He wanted to know more of what she and Nick had talked about.

THIRTEEN

CADEE HIT THE BRAKES, STOPPED AT the stop sign on the way back to the base from Emma's house. The chicken noodle soup had hit the spot. And the popcorn. And Ava's cuddle.

"Swirly, swirly, pretty swirly skirt," Cadee sang. Then she laughed at herself as she looked both ways and continued toward the base in the light of the literal midnight sun. It was sunshiny at midnight.

Man, that kids' song was stuck in her brain. Well, at least that new *Princess and the Pea* movie had made Ava's day. As had her brand-new swirly *Princess and the Pea* pajamas. Now, the suspense movie she and Emma had watched after Ava's bedtime—that was a movie she'd . . .

What was that sound?

The weird sound droned on. Her engine? Shoot. She loved her red Kia, but she didn't randomly have money to fix the engine. Maybe Vince and Hammer would help her do it herself.

If only she had her phone. She pulled over, left the engine running, and flicked the button to open her hood. She took her flashlight out of the glove box, then got out of the car and peered in. Oh, it was just the fan belt, flipping around, almost split in half.

The hit came from behind, crashing through her skull, slamming her to the ground. She screamed even as someone grabbed her from behind, pushed her into the trunk of a car. She kicked out, fighting him, managed to get a foot in his gut, but he had a syringe.

It landed in her thigh, a sting that bled in coldness. No!

He slammed the trunk shut, and she fought the blackness.

Lost.

"Smile, Cadee. You're on *Candid Camera*."

Nick's voice woke her up. She started to open her eyes . . . yeah, no. Her head *hurt*. She didn't have to touch it to feel the lump. How long had she been asleep?

Oh, she hated this man.

She could still feel the effects of whatever drug he'd used, but she lay still. His steps echoed as he entered, and he stepped her direction.

"Get up." He nudged her with his toe, and she kicked hard at his shin, hoping he'd fall and she could run off.

But he fell over the top of her, grunted, popped up. He kicked her in the kidney. "I said get up."

Cadee pushed herself up, trying to adjust her eyes to the darkness.

Wherever this was, she was in a pole barn. A filthy one. Four walls and a door. She huffed. What a great amount of knowledge that was.

Nick chuckled. "Let's start again. Smile."

He stepped back and pulled out a burner phone, took a couple of pictures.

She wrapped her arms around her knees, dropped her face to not let him have any more pictures.

"Come on, Cadee, these pictures are just going to invite your buddy Vince to meet us here at the shooting range."

The shooting range? *God, help me.* "Thought

he was *your* buddy, that you were both people fighting for justice."

Nick grabbed her by the collar, dragged her up to her feet.

She was dizzy, nearly fell, but she locked her legs, refusing to fall. She stood for a moment . . . then he shoved her toward the far wall.

"Stay there. Don't move. We're just going to wait here until Vince shows up to rescue you."

Oh God. She was a lure. She wanted to vomit. She dropped to her knees.

"My head . . ."

Nick grabbed her ponytail and yanked her head back, whispering into her ear. "You will not be rescued if Vince doesn't receive these pictures. Stand up, Cadee dear."

She would never draw a teammate into this trap.

No. She wouldn't draw the man she loved into this wolf's lair.

The man she'd never stopped loving.

What do I do, God?

Her hair wrapped tightly in his fist, Nick pulled her up against the wall.

God, You helped me last time. Help me now.

"If you move, I will shoot you."

Nick's laugh filled the pole barn as he stuck

his gun in his waistband and stood back in the doorway. He lifted up his phone, snapped three pictures. Four.

Humming, Nick slid the phone into his pocket. Then he wiped the gun with the hem of his shirt and set it down on the chair just inside the door.

He threw a rope around the truss closest to the door and worked with it, pulled it tight into a noose. Her belly curdled.

He was going to hang her.

Her knees started to collapse.

He dropped a dirty, bright orange face mask under the chair. Like it had been left in a hurry.

Weird.

"You're with the militia?" she asked.

He threw back his head and laughed, spun on his heels. "Have fun, Cadee," he said cheerfully as he closed the door.

Snaps of a padlock locking the door jolted her brain into action. Light bled around the edges of the door, but there were no windows, no obvious way out.

She glanced at the gun. Why had he left it behind? She stood up on the chair to pull the noose down from the truss, but it was too tight. She jumped down.

A noose *and* a gun to kill her didn't make

much sense. But it was clear why Nick had taken pictures of her—to lure Vince here to save her. Probably so he could kill them both.

Nick wanted her dead *and* Vince as well. So he could continue to pin all those crimes on a man who was supposed to be his friend?

She squatted down next to the face mask and fingered it, thinking about the militia and how they'd shot at them. Twice. Men who trained and practiced at this shooting range. Yet they'd missed. Both times. They had just been trying to scare them away.

She threaded the face mask through her fingers, unthreaded it. Thanks to this, it would look like they'd set up a murder-suicide scenario.

She tossed aside the face mask, wrapped her arms around her knees, dropped her face to her knees. *I'm sorry, Vince.*

That talk they'd been going to have later?

That was what she wanted—to bring it all back between them. Their friendship. The joy of their romance that had never gone away, despite all the fighting they had fallen into.

A dim smile crossed her face. Sometimes that rivalry was kind of fun. A challenge.

She loved him.

She hadn't known he'd been a DEA agent. But

she did know something else—especially after he'd landed on top of her in the salmonberries: he was as passionate for justice as he was for rescuing people.

She loved him.

The brightness in his dark eyes.

The sweaty hugs after a workout at Ember training camp.

The way he'd shared his father.

Yeah. She loved him.

God, give Vince and me a chance at that talk later. Please. Just give us a chance. Get me out of here.

A padlock jiggled. Nick checking that she was still locked in. She wrapped her arms back around her knees.

I love Vince, God. Keep him away from this wolf he used to think he could trust. Nick wants to kill him.

And her.

She wanted to cry. Absolutely wouldn't. She wiped her face.

Suddenly she heard the loud crack of bolt cutters. She stood, ready to fight for her life.

The door flew open, and five men burst in wearing hunting clothes and ball caps, guns hanging from their shoulders.

Militia, of course. The same bright orange face masks as the guys who'd shot at her and Vince after the plane crash. If she remembered right, Landon had had the same one twisted around his neck at the salmon die-off creek they'd fallen into.

And been shot at.

"What are you guys doing?"

"Shut up," the black-haired guy said as he grabbed her by the arm and pulled her out. Her eyes watered a bit in the Alaskan sun.

Two others stood outside the pole barn, holding Nick between them, who was struggling to escape. He saw her and redoubled his efforts.

The black-haired leader popped him on the side of his head. "Stop it. What did you think was going to happen when you got the government interested in us?"

"I'd never . . . it was just that—"

"Shut up. You know Viper needs to talk to you."

One of the guys pulled out duct tape. He taped Nick's mouth shut, then hers, took Nick's phone, patted her down for hers. Except she didn't have it.

The tape guy took a step back and nodded to the guys holding Nick and the man holding her. They pushed her toward some ATVs.

The black-haired guy walked backward, his gun at the ready, and looked from her to Nick, then back to her. "Thanks to you, she knows too much too."

By the next morning, Vince still hadn't shaken the feeling that something might be wrong.

He walked over to the mess hall's coffee area, refilled his mug, then stepped outside to watch for Cadee. He looked out over Copper Mountain, Denali, all the foothill mountains. Denali was still bright with snow, but Copper Mountain, not as high, was a rich green.

Cadee would want him to say something about God being an awesome creator.

Maybe he would.

He flexed his fingers, took a sip of coffee.

She hadn't come for that talk after her shower last night. She hadn't even come just for coffee this morning. He loved that woman, and they had a future. He wanted that talk with her. Maybe they could take a walk, somewhere where the rest of the team wouldn't be.

But that wasn't what was bothering him.

The hum running through his fingers—it would happen back in his DEA days.

Something was wrong.

"Good morning, Vince." JoJo waved as she walked past him to go into the mess hall.

"Good morning, JoJo. Hey, is Cadee up yet?"

"Not sure. I haven't seen her. No one's in the women's cabin though. She's not in the mess hall?"

"Nope. She told us last night she was going to watch movies at her sister's house. She must have stayed overnight."

She chuckled. "Hope Ava went to bed and the women got to watch something other than kids' movies."

As the door closed behind her, he debated whether texting Cadee would seem pushy. But he wanted to see her, he wanted their talk.

He pulled the phone out of his pocket. Maybe he'd just check it.

A text popped up on his screen.

Emma
_____
Hey, Vince. It's Emma. Have you seen Cadee? She always texts me when she gets back to the base after one of our movie nights. I called and texted several times. But she didn't respond to me last night or this morning. I'm a touch worried.

He thumbed one back.

> _____ Vince
> Hey, Emma. I'll let you know
> as soon as I find out, but I'm
> assuming everything is all okay.

He added a winkie face emoticon to reassure her and Ava. Cadee had never shown up last night? That meant wherever she was, she could be in big trouble.

But he was more than a touch worried. Way more than a touch.

He popped his head back into the mess hall. Most of his team sat eating or drinking coffee. He walked over to the group. "Anyone see Cadee last night? This morning? Emma's looking for her."

They all shook their heads. Jade looked at her phone, shook her head again.

"Join us," he heard one of them say. But his thoughts were starting to gel. Emma didn't know where she was. JoJo had said everyone was out of the women's cabin. And none of the rest of the team had seen her either. He knew himself that the men's cabin was empty too. The married couples' cabin was locked up.

His phone buzzed, and he glanced at it. He'd normally just hit delete on a text from "Anonymous," but his fingers hummed. Maybe the text below Emma's was actually from Cadee for some reason. He clicked on it.

His stomach dropped to his feet.

Pictures of Cadee . . . injured. In some small building he didn't recognize. A pole barn with a high, narrow window, so not much light. Trusses. Nothing more than a storage room. One door. One chair where Cadee sat, her eyes looking bleary. She had to have been drugged.

And the message with it sent chills.

> Anonymous
> With me. Now. Chulitna River
> Shooting Range. Don't bring
> anyone if you want her alive.

That had been sent a half hour ago.

He exploded out of the mess hall, the door slamming behind him. He sprinted over to the men's cabin. His breaths raked his chest.

He grabbed his go bag, then he ran to his SUV.

But the entire team had run out to the lot. Skye and JoJo sat on his fender, Logan leaned up against the driver's side door.

"Blocking me from leaving?" he rumbled. "Cadee is in trouble."

Jade nodded. "What's going on? She's our team member too. You looked pretty freaked out when you took off."

"I got a text. Someone has grabbed her—but I have to go *alone*." He shoved his phone at her.

She took it, and he could tell when she saw what he had seen. She paled. "I see." She looked at the pictures for a minute as she decided what to do. "Hey, everyone, Cadee is injured. Pretty badly as far as we can see. She's at the Chulitna shooting range. We're going to back up Vince, even though the message—of course—says for him to show up alone."

Logan's set jaw, JoJo's furrowed eyebrows . . .

Skye held up her phone from her position on the fender. "I already texted Rio. He's on the way with Jared Jensen."

"The trooper," Vince growled.

"You ought to respond to this text while we wait for them—and we *will* be waiting for them."

She met his gaze, unwavering.

"You're going to get her killed."

"No, we won't." Her jaw tightened. "We'll stay out of sight, but we're a team, Vince. You know that. We're in." She slapped his phone back into his hand.

He looked around at his team. These people he cared about, relied on, were here to help him find Cadee. Like Jade had said.

"Thanks for having Cadee's back, everyone," he said.

"And yours," Skye added with a sideways grin.

His throat clogged up, so he just nodded his head. He confirmed that he was on his way and hit Send.

Sirens mourned in the distance, and dust flew up behind Rio's station wagon as it pulled in.

Rio and Jared jumped out, jogged over.

Jade put her hand on Vince's shoulder. "They're here to help us," she said softly.

Rio ran up. "What's going on?"

"Vince got a text from someone who has Cadee," said Skye.

"Let me see." Rio held out his hand. Vince handed the phone over.

Rio studied it with Jared looking over his shoulder.

"Militia," Jared said. "This looks like the pole barn at Chulitna River Shooting Range. We've had our eyes on it for a couple months, gathering info, because a couple people working there seem to be leaning heavily toward the militia."

Vince was surprised at the growl in his voice. "I'm certain it's Nick Atwood. The *With me* in the message . . . just like him when we worked together."

Rio thumped him on the shoulder. "Nick, militia, whatever. We will unravel that. Later."

Vince gritted his teeth. *Later.* The word he'd used to put off things with Cadee.

"Right now, we have to find Cadee," Rio said.

"No, *me*. He doesn't want law enforcement to show up. Just me."

"With your DEA training, you know he wouldn't say that unless he was after *you*. Midnight Sun will lose both of you." Rio's eyebrows rose as he and Vince silently challenged each other.

Vince pursed his lips, crossed his arms across his chest. "I'm going in after Cadee."

"Vince, you are too close to this—"

"By myself."

"You're not going in alone."

Vince met Rio's gaze. "I am. I was DEA. I can handle myself."

Rio took a breath. "No way."

Vince made to argue, but Rio held up his hand. "We'll stay out of sight."

Oh. But maybe not a terrible idea to have armed backup. "Okay."

"Let's go, Jared," Rio said. He turned to Vince. "We'll call the troopers' office. Send them to Chulitna River Shooting Range."

The men jogged toward the SUV.

Jade yelled, "Excuse me!"

Vince slid his phone into his pocket, stood with them.

Rio stopped, turned around.

"Cadee's ours," Jade said.

"Fine. You all stay behind us."

No response.

He looked at Skye. "I'm serious." His mouth pursed, accompanied by a shake of his head. "Don't get in the way."

She held up her hands. "We're not cops."

"Don't forget that." He got into his truck.

Logan, Skye, and Jade piled into the back of his truck, and Vince jumped in behind the steering wheel. They took off, leaving dust behind them as they drove to the main road.

Please, God, don't let Nick hurt her. Apparently, now, he was all about praying.

Why not? What other choice did he have?

About a half mile away from the shooting range, he came up to where Rio and Jared had parked a little way back from the entry.

Vince rolled down his window, and Rio walked up, his eyes widening at the sight of the Midnight Sun team in the back.

"They promised to stay behind us, and they promised they know they're not cops."

Rio sighed. "Okay then. Jared and I are going in with you. We'll get out before you reach the gate."

He nodded. "Whatever happens, get Cadee out of there."

Rio's mouth tightened, but he nodded. He and Jared sprang into the back of the truck.

Vince pulled to a stop just outside the gate under the arch that crossed the driveway. Rio and Jared jumped out, knelt by Vince's window. "We'll climb over," Rio said. "Two pole barns. Right next to each other."

Vince popped out of his truck, glanced at the SJs waiting in the back. He knelt next to Rio and Jared. "I'll listen at each, find which one she's in."

"I'll check the office building," Rio said, "then stash myself on their east side, where I'll be able to see you."

"I'll be behind the bushes along their fence," Jared said.

Vince nodded. "When I find which pole barn Cadee is in, I'll go in. Do not deploy until I give you the signal."

"What signal is that?" Jared asked.

"I don't know." Vince looked between the two men. "But if you see Cadee, grab her and run."

Rio gave him a tight nod. Vince got out, climbed the fence, dropped in, Jared and Rio behind him.

Vince stayed low beside the first pole barn while Rio checked the office and Jared got into place.

He didn't hear anything. He ran to the second pole barn.

No sound.

She could be unconscious. In either one. But there were footprints just outside the first one. Nick had obviously cleaned his footprints from the concrete pad around it.

He gave a low chuckle when he saw the rest of his team, hunkered down along the fence. So much for obeying Rio.

Please don't get hurt.

He pointed to the first pole barn, spotted Rio, who nodded.

He walked up to the door, reached his hand to knock.

God, Cadee needs You right now.

I need You.

He knocked. "It's Vince. I'm here. Ready to do whatever you want."

Silence.

He put his ear up to the door.

Silence.

He signaled the two men, and they came behind him at the door, so close he could feel their breaths.

He kicked open the door and rushed in with Rio and Jared.

The room was empty except for a chair. A noose. A gun. Nick's service weapon?

Where was Cadee?

"She's not here," Rio said, searching the barn. He came back to Vince. "They've moved her."

"How do we find her?" Jared said. "Maybe Nick has his phone. We could track him from the text you sent."

Wait. Her tracking ring—the one that Jade had given all the jumpers. "I have an idea."

FOURTEEN

THE ATV CAME TO A STOP. SHE could feel it, despite her blindfold.

A hand dragged Cadee off the four-wheeler and pushed her into a building.

This place smelled like dogs.

The door clanged, and there was yet another click of yet another padlock.

Someone said, "Okay, take off the masks."

Cadee worked off the mask, spotted Nick sprawled beside her.

They were in a dog kennel. Two German shepherds were in the kennel right next to them, running back and forth along the chain-link between them, sniffing hard, growling. The same dogs who had hunted her and Vince in the backcountry?

Hanging in the big building outside the two

huge kennels were bite sleeves, even a bite suit. Tug ropes.

Guard dogs.

"Seven semiautomatics." Nick whispered the words, pointing at the wall next to the bite suit. Two of the slots were empty though.

"Don't talk to me. You're the reason we're in this situation." She looked up. Chicken wire above them blocked their escape.

"No climbing out." Nick backed up against the chain-link opposite the dogs.

"Shut up," she whispered back.

"Hey, Clint, get in here," the middle-aged guy yelled. How could he even wear that American flag shirt when he was holding her prisoner?

A blond, twenty-something militia guy came in. "Hey, Dad." He stopped in his tracks. "What are we doing with *people* in that kennel? I don't need all four shepherds in one kennel."

"Don't worry about it. Just get those dogs under control."

"Eh, they're just sniffing around. They're fine right now." He nodded over at Cadee. "Don't put your fingers through the fence. That one looks like she'll bite."

He and his dad laughed as they walked into an office off to the side of the room. The younger man—Clint—pulled the office door shut, but not hard enough. The latch didn't click, and the door swung back open a bit.

"Dad, seriously, what are we going to do when the other two shepherds finish their tour around the compound? We can't have all four in the same kennel. They'll tear each other up."

"Don't worry." A file cabinet opened and shut. At least, it sounded like a file cabinet. "I'll help you put up the separator in a bit."

"Okay, fine."

From the next room, an office chair gave a groan. From her vantage point, Cadee spotted Clint swinging his feet onto the corner of the desk. "Aren't those the two people we were trying to get away from the new compound? What happened?"

The dad laughed. "Viper was told that woman was talking to an FBI guy and that we need to find out what she thinks she knows about us. Viper is coming, so we need answers before he gets here."

Nick touched Cadee's shoulder, cut his voice to a whisper. "Let's get out of here."

She gave him a glare.

"That skinny guy in there with the long face and fake fur collar on his jacket—he's trying to build some tourist recreation that we don't want around here. Boss is eager to meet him," the dad urged.

Well, Nick was creepy, but he was right. They needed to get out of here. Before the boss showed up. She started walking around the tiny enclosure. Nick walked the opposite way around.

The dad snorted. "Feed Gunner and Cobra. Get them ready for their tour. Is Nathan ready to walk it with you?"

"Of course he is." He swung his legs off the desk and walked out of the office. He pulled out steaks and fish from the mini fridge on the counter, then began to cut the steaks into bites.

"Dad, none of this fish came from that die-off river, right?"

"Of course not. Can't believe Landon dumped that much chemical into the one river. We're going to get attention."

"I know, right? Viper isn't happy at all, but Landon always says 'Waste is waste.'" Clint tore up the fish, put some into each bowl. The dogs were running back and forth, whining, drooling, eager for the food. "Dogs sure love themselves some fish."

His dad laughed. "Boy, do they."

"I don't see any way out," Nick said quietly, behind Cadee.

Clint reached up into the upper cabinet, pulled out two chewy treats. He walked over to the dogs, lifted the cover over the wide, tall feeding slot in the door. He tossed one of the treats in with a chuckle. "That'll keep you calm until I'm done with your dinner." Then he walked over to Cadee and Nick's enclosure. "Sit down."

Cadee backed away from the chain-link, looking for security cameras. She'd give a sign, hope Vince somehow hacked into it. How would he even know to hack into it? Well, it was worth a try. And a prayer.

Nope. No security cams for militia with guard dogs, apparently.

The two dogs pounced into a wrestling match over one of the chewies. "Stop it," Clint shouted at them. He returned to the counter to finish preparing their meals.

What else could she do?

The dad's phone went off in the office. "Michael here . . . Hey, Viper. So you're headed our way?" He stood and slammed the door to the office shut.

Clint scratched his nose, tilted his head at the rack of guns beside the office. "See? Viper is on his way in. Talk to him if you've got questions." He snickered and followed his dad into the office, leaving the food on the counter. Another door slam.

"If they hadn't taken my gun, we'd be out of here. We need to talk over this situation, Cadee," Nick said.

She spun around. "We've talked enough already. Remember when I had to basically jump out of your car? You're done."

He pushed Cadee back, and she fell to the ground, snapped up to her feet again, her back against the wall. "If we don't work together to get out of here, neither of us will escape."

Something bumped up against the outside of the wall. She jumped away. Stood stock still in the middle of the enclosure.

Footsteps. Outside. And the murmured sounds of talking.

She started breathing hard. Was this the boss Clint had talked about? Militia coming in after them? She didn't want to meet a guy named Viper!

"We need to get out of here. Now," he said, clearly hearing them too.

Agreed.

She had watched the guy feed the dogs a treat in the next kennel, and Cadee and Nick's door had a feeding slot too. Wide and deep enough for her arm. She pushed it open and snaked her hand up to the lock. Just a slide lock the dogs had no chance of using—but this kennel wasn't built to contain a person. She slid it open, and the door swung wide with a bang.

Nick pushed past her, and she let him. No way would she follow him. She was getting out of here.

She took off for the door just as the dad smashed out of the office. He grabbed a gun off the wall and shouted, "You aren't going *anywhere*."

They crept up, whispering instructions, to the concrete building where Cadee's tracker ring had led them. Vince pointed at the two doors on the building, and Rio stood on guard outside the front door while Jared stood at the other.

Logan had stationed himself just outside the compound, sneaking in behind Vince. Hopefully, they could grab Cadee and run.

He didn't need the SJs, but Logan, Jade, and Skye had insisted on coming after Cadee with them, leaving the rest fighting the fire that had exploded just outside of Wasilla.

What on earth? A hollow whir zoomed above him. He glanced up. Oh. Jade had apparently brought her drone. Eye in the sky.

Rio stood beside the door, hand in the air, silently counting down from three. Jared twisted himself in front of the door, shouted, "Law enforcement!" Battered in the door with the flat of his foot.

Vince charged in, Rio and Jared right behind him.

A militia guy held Cadee at gunpoint.

And Nick was just behind Cadee.

They both held their hands in the air, and the militia guy pivoted the gun between the two of them.

Vince moved to knock Cadee against the floor and throw himself over her, but Rio aimed his gun at the guy.

Vince stopped, basically in the center of the room, looked around. A kennel held two dogs, barking, snarling, bashing themselves against the chain-link walls of the kennel, saliva dripping from their jaws.

"Vince!" Cadee shouted. Ignoring the man's gun, she barreled toward him.

Vince threw himself at the old man, tackled him, knocking the gun away.

The man rounded, kicked Vince in the shoulder, and he stumbled back.

"Stay down!" Rio shouted.

Nick had grabbed Cadee by the hair and pulled her to himself. He dragged her to the dog equipment shelves on the opposite wall and pulled a gun out of a box on the shelf—the gun with the handle customized with NA in pearl. Nick's personal revolver.

The older militia guy roared. "Clint, release the dogs."

The younger guy ran past him toward the kennel, but Jared slid in front of the enclosure, aimed his gun at Clint. The dogs rammed against the chain-link, rattled at it, bit at it, trying to get at him. "Stay where you are," Jared ordered.

"Calm down!" Nick shouted. Vince's gaze snapped back to Cadee. She was twisting herself hard in the crush of Nick's arms, kicking at him. Rio's gun remained steady on the militiaman.

The older man lunged for his gun, still in the dirt.

Rio squeezed off a shot.

"Dad!" Clint raced to the older guy, falling to the floor beside his father. "No, no, no!"

Jared aimed at Clint now. But he didn't shoot.

Wiping tears, Clint glared around at them. "You killed him."

Vince sidled up behind Clint and grabbed his arms before he could rise. He pulled the guy up and padlocked him in the other kennel. The kid sank to the ground, hid his face in his knees.

Vince turned to Nick.

Nick looked between Rio and Jared. "You guys aren't going to shoot me. You'll hit your precious Cadee. Let us through. Then I'll let her go. All good."

His gaze landed on Vince.

Vince shook his head. "You were my trainer. You taught me to never trust the hostage taker."

Nick laughed. "Wow. You didn't lose your DEA training."

Vince nearly stormed him. Nearly launched himself at him. But a look from Rio—and frankly, his own training—stopped him.

He leaned casually back against the chain-link enclosure. "Nick, we're friends. Best if you tell *me* what was going on. Before backup gets here."

"Ah. De-escalation," Nick said.

"I don't get it. We worked well together, had each other's backs. I thought we were friends."

Nick raised a shoulder.

"But now you're holding my girlfriend hostage." He shook his head. Cadee's eyes flashed.

Yep. Girlfriend.

He winked at her.

In his peripheral vision, Rio and Jared inched closer and closer to Nick.

"Nick, how's Beth? I haven't seen your wife in a long time."

Nick shook his head. "Living big, of course. Why I love her."

Vince smiled. "I bet so. Not a lady to say no to." Which was likely at least part of the reason Nick was in this situation.

Nick chuckled. "Yep. I bought her the cheapest house in the best neighborhood. Fixed it up. I won't let her lose it."

"You didn't buy that house for Beth. You bought it for the two of you."

Nick nodded, pulled Cadee's ponytail tight.

She winced. "What does Beth do, Nick?" Smart question, to get the man's mind off Cadee and onto his own life. Smart to use her name. A lot.

"She started a thrift shop. People love to come to it in our upmarket neighborhood—expensive clothes at a discount." He looked over at Rio and Jared, noticed they'd been sneaking up to him. He jammed his gun into Cadee's ribs. "Won't let her lose that either."

Vince pretended he didn't see the gun digging into Cadee's ribs. De-escalation. "Man, I don't blame you." He grinned. "Beth's chicken-mush-room lasagna is to die for. I loved eating at your place those days."

The sparest smile twitched Nick's lips. "Beth made it whenever she knew you were coming."

Yeah, then Nick had faked evidence against him. Some friend. He bit back that accusation, however.

Rio was nearly within arm's length.

"And her cheesy garlic bread with it was per-fect."

"Of course. Why would I ever eat at a restau-rant when I have Beth to cook for me?"

Vince gave him a gentle smile. "Beth . . ."

He let the silence sit heavy on Nick. Let him think of that beautiful, dark-haired woman he lived his life around.

Not Rio's and Jared's guns sneaking closer.

Not the gun he was holding.

Not Cadee.

The silence grew until he could see Nick could hardly breathe. His eyes were wide, the white showing all around the brown of his eyes. Now. "You're going to lose Beth tonight. Lose every-thing. You know this isn't going to end well."

The man's gun wavered.

Cadee must have felt it, because just like that,

she twisted out of his grasp, dropped to the ground.

Nick roared, grabbed at Cadee.

"No!" Vince shouted, his hands up. "It's me you want. For whatever reason. It's me."

Nick shifted, aimed his gun straight at him.

He nodded. "That's right."

Cadee scrambled away, then stood and sprinted to Logan, who'd appeared at the front door.

Vince boldly took another step closer to Nick's gun. They'd trained this together. *Nick* had trained him. "Why have you put this all on me? You know I didn't sign property documents. You know I haven't skimmed from the scholarship fund."

"Easy. The DEA looked at you before. They'll look at you again."

"I was innocent before. I'll be innocent again. Because I was. And am. You're going down, partner."

Nick's eyes narrowed.

"Hey," Vince said quickly, a suspicion dawning. "I was just thinking, I never did meet your friend Landon. The confidential informant you used in Cali. What's he doing up here in Alaska?" If Nick confirmed the connection, it was one more piece of the puzzle.

"Landon was an intel for me. He moved here to get away from the law. Found this militia group." He shook his head. "What a stupid choice."

"Yeah. They're pretty crazy people, aren't they?"

"Pretty smart. Funded. Connected like you wouldn't believe."

Logan had disappeared with Cadee and now peeked in the side door, pointed his thumb toward the end of the long driveway.

So the DEA was just up the road. And with Cadee out of trouble, this was ending. But not without explanations. "What are they up to here, Nick?"

His sudden laugh echoed through the building. "They're good with chemicals."

Vince's head jutted forward in surprise. "Really?" He took a step closer. A second step. So did Rio from the left. Jared from the right.

The crazy laugh stopped. "You'll see."

Nick's eyes flicked over to Rio, and Jared took advantage of that to also step closer. This conflict was mushrooming.

Vince looked at Rio and Jared and hoped his best friend—his former best friend—wouldn't die. Even if he had set Vince up.

Just like he hoped Cadee wouldn't die. Prayed

she wouldn't. He so wanted to try again at a future with her.

His breath caught in his throat.

They would fight for that future together, and that future was all about God.

Because everyone deserved a second chance.

"Come on, Nick. You wanted in on this awesome chemical project. You heard about it from Landon and manipulated the situation. Didn't you? For Beth. You and Beth both live big."

Vince caught the gazes of Rio and Jared, and they stepped forward. Again.

Nick's mouth twitched. His eyes never left Vince's. They were so red-hot it was obvious he wanted to turn him into a pile of ash. Then he swung his arm and aimed at Jared, but Rio kicked Nick's arm from behind as he pulled the trigger. Jared jumped and grabbed his shoulder.

The gun hit the floor and spun away.

"Just a graze," Jared called. "Just a graze!"

Vince launched at Nick, tackled him to the ground.

Nick tried to throw him off, but not this time. Vince put a knee into Nick's back. "Stay. Down!"

Nick writhed, trying to escape, but Vince grabbed his arm, forced it back into an arm bar. Nick had taught him that too.

Nick cursed.

And Rio was right there, forcing Nick's arms behind his back. He handcuffed him.

Vince rolled off him.

"I'm one hundred percent sure the rest of the militia team fled the compound when they heard the guns in here," Jared mumbled.

"Hundred percent," Rio said. "Calling Davis." He headed to the dog kennel with handcuffs, where Clint had just crumpled in the corner and not moved since the death of his dad.

Jared rubbed his shoulder, pulled out his phone. "Calling AST."

"And an ambulance," Rio said, pointing at the spot on Jared's shirt where the blood from the bullet graze still glistened.

Jared rolled his eyes, nodded.

Vince squatted, breathing, panting.

Cadee.

He stood up, jogged outside. There she was . . . at the truck talking to Logan.

Logan winked at him, moved to the van where Jade was steering her drone back to them.

He ran over to Cadee, scooped her up into a kiss. "I love you."

Cadee took a deep breath with a grin. "That

thing we were going to talk about—never mind. I love you too."

And she kissed him. Or he kissed her. Whatever.

Sirens sounded in the distance.

FIFTEEN

AFTER BEING THE LAST PERSON checked out, Cadee finally walked out of the Copper Mountain clinic, waving goodbye to the doc. She'd only ended up with a piece of gauze on the side of her head where Nick had injured her. And a headache. And exhaustion.

It had taken almost all day, giving statements and everything.

She inhaled the fresh air that smelled of spruce and moss instead of dogs. Denali had a thick blanket of fog over her head, but the nearest foothill was dressed in a deep, rich green in the late-night Alaskan summer sunshine.

Wait. Where was everyone?

She looked around, and there sat Vince on the hood of that dark-bronze F-150 of his. He jumped off, wearing that one-sided grin that she loved so much.

"Hey, Cadee."

She smiled. "Hey, Vince. Where is everyone?" she asked, jogging over to his truck.

"Headed to the jump base. I told them I'd give you a ride home. And here—" He tossed her phone over to her. "They found this in Nick's truck."

Cracked screen protector. Could be worse. The whole situation could've been. "How's Jared?"

He laughed and pulled out his phone. "Here, I'll show you the picture." He poked at the phone and held it out.

Jared stood in front of the building she'd just been rescued out of—the militia's dog building— with a huge, goofy, show-off grin, pointing at a large gauze pad taped onto his shoulder. Cadee laughed. "Glad it was just a graze."

"It was a bit hairy in there for a bit. And it got even hairier—that chemical stuff isn't just toxic. It's lethal."

"Yikes. Glad that's not in your wheelhouse anymore."

Oh. One of his one-sided grins. "I'm glad we're in the same firefighting wheelhouse," he said.

She laughed. "Me too. That reminds me. Logan

said Tori and Orion just got back to the jump base. Full of stories."

He leaned up against the back fender of the truck. "We don't have to head back to base if you don't wa She always texts me when she gets back to the base after one of our movie nights. nt."

She sagged against the truck next to him. "Thank you, thank you. I don't necessarily want to. Everyone in Midnight Sun will keep asking me if I'm all right."

Vince grinned. "Jade said that would probably happen. So, *if* it's all right, let's head elsewhere."

"Where's 'elsewhere?'"

"Not telling you."

"Okay, except . . ." She motioned down at the jeans and T-shirt her kidnappers had messed up.

He shrugged. "So what?"

She chuckled and pushed up from the truck's fender. "Let's do it."

She leaned against the window, closed her eyes as he drove. His hand rested lightly over hers on the console between them, which inexplicably made her both relaxed and quivery. His truck was somehow comfy, and she dozed off. Deeply.

Then she startled awake, taking a moment to realize where she was.

In Vince's truck. Vince's truck?

She sat up, wiped the drool from her mouth. That was embarrassing. Vince was sitting out at a picnic table. It was like someone had made the clearing for no purpose but the table.

Fortunately, his back was to her. Cadee pulled the rearview mirror her direction, retied her ponytail. Then she pulled it out again, finger-combed her hair, and gently pulled off the gauze. That would leave a bit of a scar.

It was as good as she could do. At least the sleep had done her some good.

She climbed out of the truck, shut the door. "Hey, Vince, this is 'elsewhere?'"

Laughing, he turned around. "Glad you finally woke up. You must have needed the sleep."

She sat down across from him and glanced at her watch. "A good hour-long nap was enough to send away my headache."

Vince scooched a large travel mug across the table to her.

"Ooh. Coffee. Thanks."

"Of course." He ran his hand along the cut on her head. "Looks like it's already healing."

"Yeah." She didn't want to talk about Nick and everything that had happened. She pointed with a grin at the handle-top pastry box in the middle of the table. "What's that?"

"A plate-size cinnamon roll." He waggled his eyebrows. "Genevieve's Bakery."

"And I thought she was all about baking cookies for Copper Mountain." Cadee opened the box, sniffed deeply of the rich cinnamon. Her stomach grumbled, and she pulled off a hunk, took a bite. "This is the best. Where are we?"

"This is the backroad between Copper Mountain and Denali. Nice drive from the base. No clue at all why this picnic bench is here, but it is. Dad and I discovered it one week when I came up for a visit during college spring break. Cinnamon roll and coffee every morning we could. Haven't been here since he passed." But he smiled.

"What did you guys talk about?"

"Parachuting. College professors. Cinnamon rolls. The Bible. Jesus." He took a sip of coffee. "My future."

Silence fell comfortably between them as she sipped her coffee too and ate another piece of the roll. But she had a question that wouldn't quit niggling. "Vince, I guess what I have never understood is why you broke up with me. At the funeral."

He grimaced. "I did, didn't I?" She nodded, and he leaned forward, took her hands in his.

"Dad was a good man." He paused, as if trying to pull his thoughts together.

"Cap *lived* his faith, shared it," she said.

"Exactly. I didn't want to disrespect him by hating God for taking him away. No, let me correct that. I didn't want to disrespect *God*. So when Dad died, I just went neutral."

She rubbed her thumb along the side of his hand. "That also explains the break-up. And the fighting."

"Instead of real conversations." He pulled away his hand. "Did I tell you I've started praying?"

"You have?"

"Surprised myself. But I've sort of realized that I don't want to be detached from God."

"What do you mean?" She popped another bite of cinnamon roll in her mouth.

"I mean that my relationship with God is back. A real one."

She grabbed his hands, squeezed them hard.

He took a deep breath. "I can't believe I went all neutral."

"We're, you know, humans." She elbowed him.

It made him laugh. "Do this every week?"

"One hundred percent."

"We probably can't make it here every week." She sipped from her mug. "Of course not.

We're firefighters. But we need this, both of us. Coffee too."

"But, Cadee . . ." He took a breath. "What about *us*?"

Cadee got up, walked around, and slid onto the bench next to him. Her eyes crinkled with a smile. "We're great. It blew me away that you came to rescue me."

"Why? I love you."

His hands on either side of her chin, he leaned in, kissed her. Until they could hardly breathe. Then they gazed into each other's eyes.

"So, no more fighting? No more bossing me around?"

He grinned, and with it came the heat of the summer, the fresh breeze of their tomorrows.

"Let's not go that far."

And then he kissed her again.

BONUS EPILOGUE

Thank you for reading *Burning Rivals*. We hope you loved this story. Find out what happens next for Cadee and Vince with a **Bonus Epilogue**, a special gift, available only to our newsletter subscribers.

This Bonus Epilogue will not be released on any retailer platform, so get your free gift by scanning the QR code below. By scanning, you acknowledge you are becoming a subscriber to the newsletters of Voni Harris, Lisa Phillips, and Sunrise Publishing. Unsubscribe at any time.

THANK YOU

Thank you so much for reading *Burning Rivals*. We hope you enjoyed the story. If you did, would you be willing to do us a favor and leave a review? It doesn't have to be long- just a few words to help other readers know what they're getting. (But no spoilers! We don't want to wreck the fun!) Thank you again for reading!

We'd love to hear from you—not only about this story, but about any characters or stories you'd like to read in the future. Contact us at www.sunrisepublishing.com/contact.

READ ON FOR MORE FROM

CHASING FIRE:
ALASKA

Gear up for the next Chasing Fire: Alaska
romantic suspense thriller, *Burning Escape*
by Lisa Phillips and Michelle Sass Aleckson.

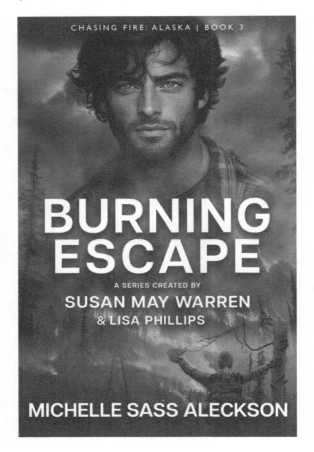

RESCUE. DANGER. DEVOTION. THIS TIME, THEIR HEARTS ARE ON THE LINE.

He was born to fight fires...

When Tori Mitchell said goodbye to the handsome stranger after their heart-stopping dance on her last night of freedom, she never expected him to wind up on the same Midnight Sun elite smokejumper team. Now the two rookies are on the run through the Alaska backcountry, chased by militia men intent on stopping the wildlands firefighters. Forced to rely on each other, Tori has to ignore the sparks between them if they're going to stay alive. Otherwise that spark will turn into a flame neither of them can put out.

He's got something to prove...

Born into a family legacy of firefighting, Orion Price is determined to prove his worth up in Alaska. One explosive evening on the dance floor with Tori threatens the only shot he has to step out of the shadow of his mistakes. He's going to take this shot to show his family— and himself—that he can be the man they believe he is. Orion won't risk his heart, even if survival in an isolated community means faking a relationship with Tori.

Brace yourself for a high-octane, heart-pounding, inspirational thrill ride filled with real-life heroism, searing romantic suspense, and the restorative power of unrelenting grace.

Eight weeks earlier

HE'D MADE IT. AFTER YEARS OF dreaming, all the training, and months of planning, Orion Price was finally ready for his shot at fulfilling the heroic legacy of Grandpa Jack.

Alaska was definitely cooler than Ember, Montana. A different ridgeline loomed in the distance rather than the mountains of the Kootenai National Forest Orion knew by heart, having grown up in their shadow. Here, Denali's peak soared above the neighboring summits. Impressive, no doubt. A little intimidating . . . but mostly it sparked excitement for the adventure ahead. The adventure he'd been waiting for since he was a kid.

Orion stepped into the Midnight Sun Saloon, the smell of meat, smoky and spicy, making his mouth water. Usually a day of traveling—flying from Bozeman to Seattle to Anchorage, plus the two-hour drive to Copper Mountain—would make for a long day, but the way adrenaline was surging through him, he was ready for a good meal and to let off a little steam. He had something to celebrate.

He must not be the only one. Live music from a band out on the patio traipsed in on the breeze through an open window.

Orion found a seat next to Logan Crawford at the bar. The woman serving took his order for wings and a beer without fuss or chitchat. Within moments, a tall lager in an iced glass was plopped down in front of him. He took a long, slow sip, savoring the cold drink.

He'd put in his time with the Jude County hotshot team. He was ready for smokejumping. He just had to get through the training and nab one of the open rookie spots. He glanced at Logan next to him. His buddy from Montana had snagged an open spot on the team already, showing up at the last minute before the season began. He'd been a smokejumper in Ember and had even done a stint fighting bushfires in Australia. While Orion had grown up at Wildlands Academy learning all about fighting wildfires, he was still pretty young.

But he knew what he wanted, and he would do whatever it took. His mom—his only family for most of his life—was finally settled and now had Charlie and Orion's new half sister Alexis nearby. It gave him the freedom to spread his wings now, knowing she was happy and fulfilled.

This was his time. Finally.

A loud cry rose from the rowdy group at the other end of the bar as the bunch of bearded men downed shots. They were dirty, a little scruffy, and looked like they'd stumbled out of the wilds for a good time and didn't care much who they disturbed with their ruckus. The tall guy in the middle of the pack threw back another shot and howled at the ceiling while his buddies laughed and slapped him on the back.

"Hey, pipe down, boys. Some of us want to hear the music," the bartender yelled over her shoulder.

"Sure thing, Vic," one of the guys said with a fake smile. Then he turned back to the group and rolled his eyes.

Logan chatted with a couple of women sitting on the other side of him. Orion had never been great at flirting. Might as well let Logan charm the ladies. Instead, Orion turned on his stool to take in the view of the mountains.

His eye caught a petite blonde woman walking

toward one of the high-top tables and the two girls waving to her. As she skirted around another party, a guy in a hockey jersey was pushing away from his table.

Right into the woman's path.

Orion jumped off his seat in time to catch her as her foot caught on the chair. She grabbed his arms before she could hit the ground.

She blew a strand of long blonde hair out of her face, and he caught her wide-eyed gaze.

Wow.

Talk about Alaskan beauty. She didn't have that fake look of a lot of makeup. Just a clean glow, a smattering of freckles across her dainty nose, and wide blue eyes that reminded him of a deep mountain lake. Fathomless and gorgeous.

Her surprise quickly melted into a dazzling grin.

"You all right, ma'am?" he asked her, helping set her back on her feet.

"Ma'am? How old do you think I am?" She gave him a mock glare and then chuckled as she dusted off her jeans.

Heat rushed to his neck and cheeks. Oh, he was so bad at this. But she didn't let go of his arm.

And he was totally okay with that.

He grimaced. "Sorry. Where I'm from, it's a sign of respect."

"And where's that?" A flirty lilt in her voice drew him in. "You're too polite to be from around here."

Maybe he should be thanking the guy who'd tripped her.

He cleared his throat. "I'm from Montana."

"Ry, food's here!" Logan called from behind him. Right. Food. His job. This wasn't the time for distractions.

"I'd better go." He nodded to Logan and turned back to the gorgeous woman. "Don't want him to steal my dinner."

"Can't have that." She chuckled. "Thanks for the save, Montana."

He tipped his chin. "Anytime."

Well, okay then. Nothing quite said "Welcome to Alaska!" like a beautiful woman falling into his arms.

He could get used to this life.

Orion found his seat and dug into the steaming hot food waiting at his spot. His wings were spicy and sweet, the fries salty and crisp, just the way he liked them. See, this was what he'd been waiting for. Food even tasted better in Alaska. Adventure was in the air, and tomorrow he'd start his new job. His new life.

Logan didn't say much as they ate. Orion enjoyed his beer and scanned the crowd. Okay, so yes, he was hoping to catch another glimpse of the blonde elfin creature with big blue eyes that had fallen into his arms. The floral, almost woodsy scent she'd carried still stuck with him. Must be the excitement of finally stepping into his legacy. It wasn't like he believed in love at first sight or anything like it.

"Wanna get some fresh air? It's getting a little warm in here." Logan stood and dropped cash on the bar top.

"Sure."

With a full belly and half a beer still left to enjoy, Orion followed Logan to the deck outside. Some of the crowd were using the space to dance to the country-rock band. A flash of blonde hair, and Orion found what he'd been looking for.

The woodland sprite threw her head back and laughed as she twirled to the music. Her hands clapped high above her head as she swayed her hips. A few other girls joined her, each with a drink in their hands. But their eyes were clear, no one acted tipsy. Just a bunch of friends out for a good time.

"Why don't you go join them?" Logan bumped his shoulder. "You know you want to."

Why? Because he'd never been the Casanova type. And he'd grown up in the wilderness. Literally.

But after working an intense fire season together last year, he and Logan knew each other pretty well. Orion didn't feel the need to keep up pretenses—especially with a fellow believer who might be his roommate for the summer. "I wouldn't know the first thing about how to do that. And I have no clue how to dance."

"That's all that's stopping you? Dude, you fight wildfires. This is easy. You go out, ask the woman to dance, and feel the beat. Figure out the rest as you go."

Orion watched them another moment. The sun glinted off the woman's blonde hair as she spun. She was the picture of light and beauty and freedom.

"Go, Tia!" one of her friends called as she gave her a high five.

Tia.

The name fit. Confident and cute and . . .

My goodness, he'd just met the woman. What was wrong with him?

Okay, yes, he wanted to dance with her.

"If it's so easy, why aren't you out there?" He glanced at Logan.

His smirk dimmed. "That's not why I'm here."

"Why *are* you here? All winter, you never said anything when I brought up the fact that I was moving here. Then you call me up out of the blue and tell me you're joining too."

"I didn't know then."

"Know what?"

"That she was coming here." Logan finished the last bit of his drink.

"So there's a woman involved."

"Isn't there always?" Logan looked out past the patio lights at the mountains guarding the town, his usually jolly mood suddenly somber.

"What's her name?"

"Jamie Winters." He turned to Orion. "If you like this woman, ask her to dance. Don't let the moment pass by. You might not get another chance." He clapped him on the shoulder as he stood. "I'm going back to the hotel. Training starts at zero six hundred."

But with the Alaska sun still high in the sky, no hint of setting just yet, Orion was reluctant to join him. "I'll just finish my beer."

Logan gave him a knowing nod and left.

After one more song and finishing his own

drink, Orion still debated. Really, he should leave. He didn't need any distractions. Not now that his goal was within reach. He stood. One more glimpse couldn't hurt though.

There she was. Still dancing. But her friends were gone.

And the rowdy group of guys from the bar swooped in.

The big guy in woodsy camouflage, their leader, wrapped a beefy arm around the woman. "A little thing like you shouldn't be alone on the dance floor."

She swatted his arm away. "Get lost. I'm not alone."

"Sure looks like it." He moved in again. The woman pulled away, but one of the camo pack snuck behind and blocked her in.

That was it.

Orion jogged over. "Hey, honey, sorry I'm late." He flashed a big grin and held out his hand, wanting to give her a choice.

She hesitated a moment. Looked him in the eye, almost as if she was trying to discern his worthiness as a rescuer.

A second later, a bright smile lit the whole dance floor, and her warm hand was in his.

"It's about time, Montana. I've been waiting all night."

Tori Mitchell had one night of freedom and letting loose before another intense summer, and she was going to make the most of every second of it.

This was her year. She was going to make that smokejumper team no matter what. And chances were good. She was in the best shape of her life. She'd trained all winter. Sacrificed so much.

So for this one evening, she'd forget about the strict discipline she used to keep everything in order and instead enjoy herself, having finally accepted the invite to go out to the Midnight Sun Saloon. She'd listen to the band play and let the music move her instead of holding back like she usually did.

And she certainly wouldn't let some jerk on the dance floor ruin her night.

"Hey, honey, sorry I'm late." Montana, the handsome stranger in the navy shirt and flannel, held out a hand to her. His blue-eyed gaze locked in on her. He'd caught her earlier, blushed when she'd teased him about calling her ma'am. He had a nice Captain America vibe going on—if the Cap had come from the wilds of Montana instead of NYC.

Her hero could totally take Camo Man on with those wide shoulders, but he was trying to defuse the situation and rescue her.

She could take care of herself. But maybe for this one time it would be okay. She didn't want to fill out a police report on her one night off.

"It's about time, Montana. I've been waiting all night." She gave him her warmest smile and was finally able to pull away, since Camo released his hold on her arm.

Even if his foul breath hadn't been enough to warn her, she'd made enough mistakes with men to steer clear of someone like him.

Montana, on the other hand, was probably too good for the likes of her. He followed her lead to the other side of the dance floor. The music slowed.

He bent down. "I think the coast is clear. You don't really have to dance with me. I only wanted to help."

Yup. He was definitely out of her league.

But her mouth didn't know better.

"I came here to enjoy the music tonight." So what harm could it do to dance a little under the stars? Especially with a cute guy with dark hair falling in wild waves across his forehead. A guy who blushed.

Besides, he was probably another tourist passing through who she'd never see again.

"So maybe you could help me out?" she asked him.

"Of course. How?" He looked so sincere.

"Like this." She faced him and lightly looped her arms around his shoulders. They were nice shoulders. He wasn't big and bulky, but he was definitely fit, maybe worked out, the way his biceps bulged in the dark-blue T-shirt and flannel he wore.

He cleared his throat and dropped his head, spoke in her ear. "I, uh, I . . . don't really know how to dance."

How refreshing to find a guy who could admit he *couldn't* do something. His eyes were honest and true. And that slight flush to his cheeks only made the blue-green flecks stand out.

"That's all right. Just follow my lead." She placed his hands on her hips, where his light touch warmed her through.

"Yes, ma'am." He swallowed, looked her in the eye, and gave her a bit of a shy smile.

Oh, she could fall for this one. Sweet and polite. And he did, in fact, follow her lead as they swayed to the crooning from the stage with a soulful fiddle accompaniment. The kind of song made for luring people to fall in love.

But it was only for tonight. So no danger of that.

She moved a little closer to him, the solidness and heat drawing her in, a hint of amber and sandalwood wrapping her in a sweet embrace. "You're doing great, Montana. Who said you can't dance?"

"No one. I haven't done it before."

"Shall we take it up a notch?"

His eyebrow quirked up in a question. "Are you flirting with me?"

She chuckled. His honest question and lack of guile was refreshing. "Wow, you really don't get out much, do you?"

He sucked in a breath through his teeth. "That obvious, huh?"

"Here. Hold tight to my hand. I'm gonna spin out, and then you lightly pull me back in. Nothing to it."

"I think I can handle that."

And he did. She twirled out, her hair dancing on the cool breeze with his strong grip anchoring her. A slight tug and she spun back into his arms, rested her hand on his chest, her fingers hitting his well-defined pectorals.

He definitely worked out.

"That wasn't so hard, was it?" she asked.

A slow, lazy grin emerged on his face. "Not at all."

They danced to the next slow song, Tori tucking herself against him. The crisp spring breezes swirled through the crowd but didn't cool the air between them. The song drew to a close, the last notes floating away into the soft light of Alaskan twilight. The lead singer announced the band was going to take a little break before coming back.

"Could I . . . buy you a drink? Or a meal if you like?" He looked at her directly, a hint of vulnerability there. Not weakness by any means, but a hope that—dang—she wanted to realize for him. Looking around, she saw her friends Evie and Lucy talking with a couple of guys they knew.

Well, she *was* hungry. And it was her *one* night, so, "Sure, but why don't we get a snack to go. There's a great park by the river where we can eat." And with plenty of tourists out and about, she didn't have to worry about being too secluded.

She was rewarded with a handsome smile. They put in a to-go order for ribs and onion rings.

While waiting for their food, someone tapped

Tori on the shoulder. She turned to find one of her regulars from work.

"Hey, Damian." He looked different in jeans and a fitted shirt that showed off all his hard work at the gym. Tall and lean with dark-blond hair cut short and stylish, he had a cute brunette on his arm.

"Hey, Tori. This is my friend Amber. I was just telling her what a great trainer you are and that she should ask for you at the gym."

"Aw, that's sweet. I'm going to be gone for the summer though. But for sure come see me this fall when I'm back."

"I'll do that." Amber smiled. Damian started to ask something else, but Montana was paying for their food. Tori quickly said goodbye and turned back to the bar.

"I can pay for that." Tori started to pull out her debit card from her jeans pocket.

"No need. It's already done." His clear, steady gaze quieted the accusations and doubts. Maybe letting someone take care of her for a night wasn't so bad. As long as she didn't get used to it.

Once their food was ready, they strolled out along the main drag and headed to the riverside park.

"So, what do you do around here for work?" he asked. "Or are you on vacation?"

"I live here. But let's not talk about work. I've given myself this one night to forget about jobs and responsibilities. That's for tomorrow."

"So you're one of those live-in-the-moment kind of people?"

"Tonight I am."

He chuckled. "Fair enough. So what do I call you? At least for tonight. I thought I heard someone call you Tia?"

"I'm—" For tonight, she wanted to be someone different. Someone without her past, without the bad choices weighing her down. At least with this man, who had honor written all over him, from the way he'd rescued her on the dance floor to the fact that he'd paid for her meal. "—Victoria." She held out her hand. He shook it.

"Nice to meet you, Victoria." His hand was calloused, the shake firm, but he didn't squeeze like he had something to prove.

Wouldn't that be nice?

He didn't let go right away. "I'm Orion."

"You're named after the Greek hunter?"

"The constellation."

"Ah, so you're a star."

"Nah, just an ordinary guy from Montana with

a weird name. What about you? Are you from Alaska?"

"California."

"So what brought you up here?"

"Regrets. A man. Take your pick." She grabbed an onion ring and ripped it in half, popped a piece in her mouth. Shoot. Why had she said that? She sent him a playful wink to dispel any sense of pity that he might throw her way.

"But the joke's on him. I found a career I love. A good group of friends. I stayed, and he's gone, so . . ." She shrugged as she ate the rest of the o-ring. "So for now, Alaska is the closest thing I have to a home."

Maybe someday she'd find a place where she belonged. Her sisters kept asking when she'd settle down and find a permanent address. But like they could talk. They had both moved multiple times in the last couple years, even though now they both claimed Last Chance County was home sweet home for them.

She wiped her fingers on a napkin. "What about you? What brings you here?"

"An opportunity. I love Montana, but I wanted a chance for something bigger in a place I didn't have a history or connections. I want to be able to say I did this on my own, ya know?"

"I do. I have two older sisters that are . . . amazing, but also a lot. They practically raised me, so I kinda get it, but they are always checking on me like they don't believe I can handle myself, even though I'm grown up and have been on my own for years. So, yeah, I can respect the need to be your own person, even if it means starting from scratch."

"Exactly." His blue eyes lit with understanding . . . connection.

They enjoyed the rest of their ribs and onion rings, chatted about useless things, and listened to the frogs along the river. Tourists wandered past. The sun drifted toward the horizon.

A text notification dinged from Tori's phone. The time glared up at her from the screen. "Shoot. It's almost midnight! I should get back."

"Afraid your carriage will turn back to a pumpkin?" Orion stood to throw the to-go boxes away.

"No, I just have an early morning." A morning she needed to be at her best for. She'd worked too hard for that smokejumper spot to flounder now. "I set my alarm for midnight. I have to head back."

"I'll walk with you." Orion's dark hair, longer on top, ruffled in the wind, which had picked up. "Here." He shook off his flannel and laid it over her shoulders.

She wrapped herself up in its warmth and amber scent. She really shouldn't let herself enjoy this.

But it wasn't midnight yet.

They walked toward the saloon, a faster pace than they'd set on the way out. At one point, their hands brushed, and their fingers tangled up together. She didn't pull away. His slow smile, that slight blush, was still visible under the streetlights, and the glow of the almost full moon sent a thrill through her.

Sheesh. She was like a teenager all over again. If only she'd waited back then for a man like Orion.

They reached the edge of the parking lot at the Midnight Sun Saloon, the band music still going strong though the parking lot wasn't as full as earlier. They stopped by the road sign.

"I had a really nice night, Victoria." He still held her hand. "Would you—" He glanced down a second and then back to her eyes, a question there she didn't want to answer the way she needed to.

So she kissed him.

A sweet, simple kiss, lightly pressing her lips to his. But it heated her clear down to her toes.

Her smartwatch buzzed, killing the moment. Midnight.

She pulled back, untangled herself from him.

"This was . . . amazing, but I'm sorry. I have to go." Her night of freedom was over.

"Can I see you again?"

Oh, this was harder than she'd thought. She swallowed down a thickness in her throat. "I'm sorry, Orion, but that won't work. I only had tonight. I have to leave, and I'll be gone for quite a while."

"I'm a patient guy."

Of course he was. "No, Orion." Why were her eyes stinging? She'd just met him. And yes, he was gentlemanly and kind, but she couldn't afford any distractions.

And let's be honest, when it came to men, she had horrible luck.

"I'm leaving. I've got . . . important work to do."

"I get that, but what does that have to do with—"

"Let's just end on a good note, huh?" She grazed her fingers along his jaw and planted one last kiss on his cheek. Looking down, she caught the glint of something on his neck. A cross.

Well, that was a deal breaker right there. Good thing she was already leaving.

She turned and walked away. Didn't turn back. Didn't look.

A part of her wanted to, but there were more

important things in life. Tomorrow, she would be fighting for one of the smokejumper spots, and she couldn't let anything get in her way.

Eventually, she heard Orion's footsteps in the gravel, heading away. He wasn't following her.

Good. That was what she wanted.

She reached her little Honda Civic sitting on the other side of the lot. The parking lot light overhead glinted off a spiderweb of cracks on the windshield.

Tori whipped around, scanning the area for anyone lurking in the shadows. Who had done this?

A small piece of paper fluttered under her wiper blade.

You can't escape this time.

Orion rushed down the stairs to the lobby, too late and impatient to wait for the elevator. Today was the first step to living out his dream and doing what he was born to do.

"Dude, come on!" Logan shoved a hotel coffee into Orion's hand. "Don't wanna be late for your first day of training."

Right. Orion tried to shake off the memory of the mysterious and captivating Victoria from last night. A memory that tangled up in his head way more than he liked.

"You okay? You look awful." Logan glanced over from behind the wheel of his car.

He wasn't thrilled to have Logan following him to the Midnight Sun crew, but the guy had his own reasons for coming up here, and maybe it wouldn't be horrible to have a friend around. As long as Orion was seen as his own person.

"I'm fine. Didn't sleep great."

"Nervous?"

Sure, let Logan think that was it. "Maybe."

"You got back pretty late last night, but you're a good firefighter, Price. You've got this."

"Thanks."

Orion sipped his coffee. Ugh. Lukewarm.

So different from Victoria. She was fire and heat. And boy, had he been burned all right.

What was his problem anyway? It had been one dance. One kiss.

But it had hooked him like an expert fisherman catching a king salmon, snagging on his heart and pulling relentlessly. No other woman had done that before.

But what did it say that she'd felt no qualms about kissing him and leaving? Obviously the moment hadn't unraveled her as it had him. Maybe her job really *was* important. Or he'd simply been a distraction for her.

Whatever.

He needed his head on straight. This was his time to show everyone that he had what it took. He'd left his home, his family, everything he knew in Ember for this. He was ready to step into his legacy. And maybe redeem himself, at least a little.

They pulled into the base camp. Quonset huts, a few log-sided cabins, and a long building labeled as a mess hall all surrounded the small runway crossing through the middle of the camp. A couple of helipads and a small lot of RVs sat off to the side. The base was tucked up against foothills, out in the middle of nowhere. The crisp morning air smelled like new beginnings. Orion and Logan parked and walked into one of the open plane hangars. People milled around chatting. A small group off to the side of the room caught his eye. What in the world—

"Hey, the Trouble Boys and Sanchez are here?" Orion asked Logan.

"Guess so." Logan walked up and gave a fist bump to Hammer. "What are you guys doing here? Get too hot in Montana?"

"Something like that." Hammer grinned.

"We've been here all winter. I thought you were staying with Jude County."

"Plans changed." Logan pointed his thumb at Orion. "Thought I'd keep an eye on the rookie here. Thinks he wants to jump out of planes this year."

Orion clenched his jaw tight.

Funny. Logan didn't bring up the fact that he was here because of a woman named Jamie Winters with *these* guys. It was bad enough he thought he needed to watch over Orion. Now more of the Jude County crew were here? Who else had come up from Montana for the summer?

This was supposed to be his fresh start, a chance to work with people that didn't know him. He was supposed to do this on his own.

"You wanna be a smokejumper?" Kane asked Orion. "Between the locals and the smokejumpers from Montana, I heard there aren't many spots. We'll be joining the hotshots." The look on his face said he wouldn't have minded trying out but something had stopped him.

"Guess we'll see who gets them." Because Orion was going to nab one of the open spots no matter what. He had to. After all he'd gone through to get his mother on board with this career—which had been no easy feat, since her own father had lost his life smokejumping—he wasn't going to turn back now. At least he wasn't competing with Kane, Hammer, and the others.

A sharp whistle stopped all conversation. Everyone turned to the front of the room, where a man with a clipboard and—wait. Was that Jade Ransom? Another Jude County transplant. Seriously, had the whole crew decided to follow him here?

"I'm Tucker Newman. I'm the commander this season. This is Jade Ransom. She's jump boss, and she's running the show if you're here to train for smokejumping. If that's you, head out with her. The rest of you stick here with Mitch Bronson, who will be running the hotshot crew."

Orion and Logan and about fifteen others followed Jade out to a bay garage, doors wide open, letting the cool morning breeze in.

"Orion, good to see you." JoJo Butcher walked over to them. She ruffled Orion's hair. "You're not gonna get your pretty hair messed up jumping out of planes, are ya?"

Like he needed one more person here treating him like a little kid when he was trying to prove he was his own man. He swatted her hand away. "What are you doing here?"

"Jade is from here originally. She said she was

moving back and asked if I wanted to come. Sounded like fun, so I decided to join her."

Great.

Logan gave her a fist bump. "Good to see you."

Jade faced the group. "I'm not much of one for talking this early, so I hope you came ready to work. At the end of our training, two of you will be given a spot on my crew. Most of you have done this before, but for you newbies, this is no walk in the park. It's brutal because you are going into one of the most dangerous situations a person can face. I will push you to your limits because wildland fires don't care. Now, drop your stuff, grab one of the packs along this wall, and get ready to run."

"Good luck, newbie." Logan smirked as he grabbed one of the packs.

Orion didn't need luck though. He was born for this, so the joke was on Logan. As they lined up, Jade checked people off on the clipboard. When she got to the end of the line, she looked around. "Anyone seen Mitchell?"

After a chorus of *nos* and heads shaking, Jade blew out a short breath and made a mark on the clipboard.

Tough break, Mitchell—whoever that was. But

it was one less person vying for a place on the team. Orion smiled.

Just as they were about to start, a dusty Honda Civic with a broken windshield screeched as it swung into the parking lot.

"Wait!" a woman cried as she jumped out of the car.

Jade went out to meet her. What little Orion could see of the newcomer was weirdly familiar. But a baseball cap covered her hair, and the sunglasses she wore and Jade's shadow obscured her features.

"Must be Mitchell," Logan said. "Not a great way to make a first impression. Jade hates when people are late."

All the better for Orion.

Jade turned back to the line. "Let's go!" she yelled over her shoulder. "Mitchell, you have some catching up to do."

As Jade stepped away, slanted sunlight hit the woman, brightening her features. Blonde hair streamed behind "Mitchell's" ball cap.

Orion's smile dimmed. A force like a fist dropped into his gut.

What in the world was Victoria doing here?

"Dude, come on!" Logan nudged Orion's shoulder. The rest of the line was already running.

Orion gave himself a shake and followed Logan. He glanced back and saw Victoria rushing to heft one of the heavy packs onto her back. By the time they reached the road, she had caught up to them, though she was huffing pretty hard.

"Important work, huh?" Orion tried to take the bite out of his words, but she'd blown him off last night. Made it sound like she was leaving town or something. And now they had to compete for one of the few smokejumper spots?

Her eyes widened. "Orion?" Victoria's face was already flushed, and his name sounded more like a wheezy breath as they jogged up the inclined road with their packs. After a pause, she spoke again. "Well," she said as she huffed, "it *is* an important job. I didn't lie."

"You said you were leaving town."

"Yeah. We're gone most of the season." Each word was punctuated with another breath. "Kinda hard to do relationships that way. This is for the best. For both of us."

Or it was a lousy excuse. If she really felt that way, why had she kissed him?

But whatever. At least he knew where he stood. They weren't dating. They weren't even friends.

They were rivals competing for the same job.
One he was determined to win.

Game on.

AKNOWLEDGEMENTS

I would like to acknowledge my smokejumper and firefighter friend, who answered many questions as I wrote. He helped me lean in to an authenticity I would never have gotten close to without his help.

With a law-enforcement instructor father and a newspaper editor mother, it's no wonder **Voni Harris** grew up to write suspense novels. Voni writes from the home she shares with her legal-eagle husband on the beautiful and mysterious Alaskan island of Kodiak, where her creativity abounds. She belongs to American Christian Fiction Writers and has been published in two short-story collections: Heart-Stirring Stories of Romance, and Spiritual Citizens at http://drawneartochrist.com.

Connect with Voni at voniharris.com.

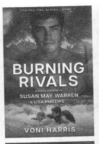

CHASING FIRE:
ALASKA

Dive into an epic series created by

SUSAN MAY WARREN
and LISA PHILLIPS

DIVE INTO AN EPIC JOURNEY IN BOOK ONE OF

CHASING FIRE: MONTANA

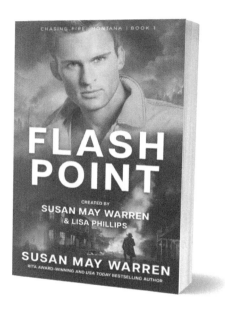

The Hollywood heartthrob and the firefighter with a secret...

What could go wrong?

Available on Amazon

LAST CHANCE
FIRE AND RESCUE

USA Today Bestselling Author

LISA PHILLIPS

with **LAURA CONAWAY**, **MEGAN BESING** and **MICHELLE SASS ALECKSON**

The men and women of the Last Chance County Fire Department struggle to put a legacy of corruption behind them. They face danger every day on the job as first responders, but the fight to become a family will be their biggest battle yet. When hearts are on the line it's up to each one to trust their skill and lean on their faith to protect the ones they love. Before it all goes down in flames.

WE THINK YOU'LL ALSO LOVE...

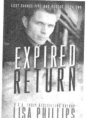

Fire Department liaison Allen Frees may have put his life back together, but getting the truck crew and engine squad to succeed might be his toughest job yet. When a child is nearly kidnapped, Allen steps in to help Pepper Miller keep her niece safe. The one thing he couldn't fix was the love he lost, but he isn't going to let Pepper walk away this time.

Expired Return by Lisa Phillips

Stunt double Vienna Foxcroft's stunt team are the only ones she trusts. Then in walks Sergeant Crew Gatlin and his tough-as-nails military dog, Havoc. When an attack on a film set sends them fleeing into the streets of Turkey, Vienna must face the demons of her past or be devoured by them. And Crew and Havoc will be tested like never before.

Havoc by Ronie Kendig

When an attempt is made on Grey Parker's life and dead bodies begin piling up, suddenly bodyguard Christina Sherman is tasked with keeping both a soldier and his dog safe... and with them, the secrets that could stop a terrorist attack.

Driving Force by Lynette Eason and Kate Angelo

We solve the problem of what we read next.   Available on Amazon

sunrise
PUBLISHING

**WHERE EVERY STORY IS A FRIEND,
AND EVERY CHAPTER IS A NEW JOURNEY...**

Subscribe to our newsletter for a free book, the latest news, weekly giveaways, exclusive author interviews, and more!

follow us on social media!

@sunrisemediagroup

@sunrisepublish

@sunrisepublishing

Made in United States
Cleveland, OH
11 June 2025